Washington Square Secrets
Book 1
Discernment

By

Carrie Dalby

One

The swaying of the southbound train
lulled me into a drowsy state against Alvin's side. I rested my head
on his firm shoulder even though the weave of his wool suit
irritated my cheek and the September heat continued to rise.

Alvin gently pressed his chin against my forehead. It was
the closest he had come yet to kissing me in public. I took
advantage of his tenderness and gazed up at him as I straightened.
His brown eyes widened a smidgeon as his square jaw fought to
remain dignified. He was serious—too serious. Alvin Robert
Farley studied patterns in geometry, football plays, and chess
matches. Never in his twenty-five years had he behaved rashly.
Never, that is, until I had cornered him into a wedding proposal
after three weeks of courting this summer of 1910.

Smiling at my husband of almost twenty-four hours, I
fingered my wedding present to him: the gold watch that looped
over a vest button on his simple black three-piece suit, and I
thought back on our night in the hotel. Now that I knew his belly
was ticklish, I planned to make him smile more often.

"Deb, don't be naughty," he glanced across the aisle to see
if our neighbors were watching my antics.

No one watched but the leering man who had startled me
when we first took our seats in Montgomery. My first thought was

he wanted to steal my bridal money, which was strapped safely to my waist beneath my clothes for the trip. Then I noticed his slit throat.

It had been weeks since I'd seen a ghost. I'd been too wrapped up in my approaching nuptials to notice the souls around me. Not caring if the vile spirit watched, I smoothed a hand over Alvin's vest and brushed my lips along his freshly shaved jaw.

"This is our honeymoon trip. I won't be denied a bit of romance when we only have a few hours alone."

Alvin blushed almost as red as the glow I could see around him. Auras were much more pleasant to deal with than ghosts. He ran a finger between his stiff collar and thick neck. "We're in a public coach."

Wanting to make him smile, not squirm, I quickly kissed his cheek. "Don't be upset that your bride finds you irresistible."

A grin broke his stoic façade. "I'd never be remiss about that. It's just…" he dropped his voice even more and put his lips by my ear. "It's not proper to display our relationship."

Wedding or not, it would take an act of God *and* Congress for Alvin to relax his standards. I nestled under his arm, and he caressed down the sleeve of my white blouse to take my hand in his.

"I love you, Deborah."

"I know you do."

I brought his hand to my lips and kissed his fingers, promising myself that one day I would assist Alvin's passion in overruling his sense of decorum. He never mentioned a previous love, but I knew he had to have at least one, if not from his youth, then his college days. He was too accomplished a kisser to not have had experience. He even had to show me how to hold my head so we could easily deepen our connection.

His calming silence allowed me to think back on the day I'd met him last autumn. Father had invited all the teachers from the boys' school he oversaw to a lawn party, as he did every year. I was raised humbly on the outskirts of the capitol city and taught that all educators were to be respected, not just the administration. As I was graduated from high school and finishing classes, I looked upon the teachers for the first time as possible contemporaries. The old-timers were as dull as ever, but the French instructor who had started the previous year eyed me with interest.

That golden afternoon was punctuated with croquet and spiced cider. Frenchie, as I called the foreign language teacher, was eager to get on my father's good side by paying me attentions. I did my share of flirting to keep boredom at bay, though I didn't deceive myself with romantic thoughts.

According to my mother, I was a quick study of people. But study was the wrong word. I knew the instant after meeting someone if they were trustworthy. It was on a spiritual level— nothing that could be observed. I credited unseen forces as my protectors because I had been saved too many times to count.

Frenchie's Louisiana roots gave him a slightly exotic air, but he was the same as any other dandy when it came down to it. During a round of croquet with Frenchie, Alvin Farley—the newest hire and former college football star—approached me with a confidant air to his athletic gait. I'd given a hearty *crack* to the yellow ball. It had missed its mark, but the sound of the connection always satisfied me. Smiling, I swung my mallet in triumph.

"Miss Alder," Alvin's deep voice had washed over me like a soothing wave, "if you took a moment to stand back and study the field, you would see the angle of your approach is all wrong."

I listened to several minutes of his polite explanations, fascinated not by his words, but his manners and the warmth coming from him when I had thought he would be a clumsy brute because of his football record.

At the close of his lecture, I smiled. "You're very thoughtful, Mr. Farley, but I'm afraid I prefer a spontaneous game. It evens the playing field when all parties are working by chance rather than against skill levels."

Frenchie had laughed, but poor Alvin looked startled. I had to work the whole school year to prove to him I was a sincere person even though my attitude was carefree. It wasn't until I approached him at the end of April with condolences over the death of his uncle—which a voice from beyond had told me about—that he really looked at me. Then it was mid-July before I was able to swindle him into taking a walk with me in the local park.

When he announced in August that he had accepted a job in Mobile and would be moving in with his widowed aunt, I knew I would lose him if he went.

"That sounds like a wonderful adventure for us," I had said.

"For *us?*" I still remember the surprise in his voice.

"I know you care for me, and I'd never survive without you, Alvin."

"You would marry me?"

I'd hugged him right there on the sidewalk in front of the soda counter. "I thought you'd never ask! Let's hurry home and tell my parents."

So, at the age of nineteen, I married the most admirable of men in a backyard ceremony on the second of September. Some would say he wasn't worthy of me, but I knew it was he who was superior. His no-nonsense, humble attitude drove me to protect him from my oddness. After all, not all young women have been speaking with ghosts since before they were school-age. Not knowing how he would handle the news confirmed my need to keep it secret.

When the train pulled into Mobile, I looked out the window in awe at the skyline. The city was larger than the capitol and featured a building over ten stories high.

Alvin buttoned his suit jacket and placed his straw boater on his head. "Come on, Deb."

I pinned my flowered hat through my brunette chignon. "Will I pass inspection with your aunt?"

"You're as pretty as a fresh magnolia, Deborah." Alvin wasn't typically an original when it came to words, but they were always sincere. He grabbed the day bag from the luggage rack. "Your complexion isn't blotchy, and your clothes aren't rumpled."

As soon as our trunks and suitcases were loaded into a hired mule cart, we headed west in an automobile from the same transportation company as the wagon. The heavy air over the city was gray with approaching storm clouds. I tried to find peace beside Alvin, but a level of unease permeated my nerves as much as the humidity caused me to glisten.

When we stopped in front of a two-story home on Rapier Avenue, Alvin escorted me up the flagstone path, my hand on his muscular arm. A charming picket fence separated the yard from its neighbors on either side. The woodwork around the porch was ornate with geometric Craftsman-style details painted a crisp white, and the busy tile on the porch floor was unlike any I'd ever seen, with tulips arranged in octagonal groups in a diamond layout.

Alvin's gaze followed mine and motioned to the flooring with his free hand. "Now that's something."

More patterns for his keen mind to dissect.

His knock on the double front door was soon answered by a woman of about thirty-five with ash blonde hair worn up and a blue lace dress adorning her curvaceous body. She theatrically flung open both narrow doors as her brown eyes took in the two of us with a sweeping glance that flickered from amused to sour before settling into a thin smile.

"Dear Alvin!" Her embrace ripped him from me with a shimmer of emerald light around her clutching form.

"Hello, Aunt Catherine." He managed to awkwardly escape her clutches and straightened his suit.

"None of that, Alvin. You must call me Cathy, the both of you." She set her eyes on me. "Now introduce me to your girl. She doesn't look old enough to marry. Are you sure you didn't steal her from the school you taught at?"

"In a way, I suppose I did. Her father was the principal." Alvin smiled and gently took my arm. "Aun—Cathy Snodgrass, this is Deborah. Deb, Cathy was married to my mother's brother, Uncle Jerald."

"You do have a bit of him in you, Alvin." Catherine took his chin between her thumb and forefinger. "That devastating jaw and dimpled chin is what first drew me to Jerald though he was a decade my senior."

Alvin blushed under her attention, and I shifted back a half-step.

"Come inside," she said.

"Our luggage should be here soon," I offered. "It might be best to wait on the porch for it."

"No, they'll knock." Catherine took Alvin by the hand and brought us over the threshold. The home was trimmed in oak woodwork with deep greens and cranberry colors on the walls and draperies. Heavy, foreboding. "Have a seat in the parlor, and I'll collect the tray from the cook."

We were motioned to the left of the entry hall while she disappeared beyond the staircase. Alvin brought me to the couch across from a fireplace flanked by two built-in bookcases.

I leaned close. "Do we have to live here?"

"She's been lonely, so you can keep her company while I'm at school."

I could think of nothing I'd want to do less than be a companion to that woman.

Catherine breezed into the room, set the tray of iced tea and refreshments on the coffee table, and took Alvin's hand. "It simply isn't fair for Deborah to monopolize you, Alvin. Come sit with me."

Too polite to protest, Alvin followed her to the sofa for two set in front of the windows.

"I'm hardly monopolizing my husband." I glanced at the mantel clock. "We've been married twenty-six hours, and he begins work in a few days. I believe I deserve every possible moment with him."

She laughed and patted Alvin's knee. "I didn't expect a two-for-one deal when you first said you were coming, but we'll make the best of things, I'm sure."

I suffered through half an hour of false pleasantries from Catherine Snodgrass. Alvin smiled politely, but he wasn't pleased with the dry cakes served. I hoped to be allowed time in the kitchen to prepare his favorite treats.

When our luggage arrived, Alvin's aunt waved us toward the staircase that had a stained glass window on the landing, another Craftsman design, bold and practically looming over us from the main floor. "Your rooms, Alvin, are the first two at the top of the stairs, where you and your parents stayed during Easter. I figured you would want a study for grading papers in the evenings, but I suppose now you'll have to take Deborah's wants into consideration."

Alvin and the delivery man carried our trunks, and then my husband followed me up with the final suitcase while I carried the round box that held my bridal hat. I set it on one of the pieces of luggage in the bedroom and took Alvin's hand.

"Let's stay here for a while," I whispered, unsure of the acoustics in the stairwell through the open doors. "We could settle in a bit."

"And a while ago you were asking not to stay." He kissed the tip of my turned up nose. "You're a strange creature, Deb."

"If we're going to be here, we might as well try to make it as much our home as possible." I motioned to the decidedly sparse bedroom set, which I did prefer to the extra fluff in the parlor. Fortunately, the mattress was a double, though I wouldn't have minded snuggling extra close to Alvin each night in a single. The blue curtains were opened, facing the towering side of the house to the south. "Everything looks functional. Did you peek in the front room?"

"Only for a moment when we set down the case of books. She's changed things since I was here when Uncle Jerald was alive, but I think you'll like the space."

He brought me through the doorway of the connecting rooms. Two windows overlooked the street above the front porch, but the heavy skies offered little sunlight that day. A lone leather wingback chair was near one of the front windows with a spindly side table beside it on the left, and a fern stand stood opposite with a lush display of greenery trailing from the basket. An empty bookcase was on the far wall, the desk situated beside it.

"It's nice, isn't it?" he asked.

I nodded. "But we'll need another chair—possibly a small chaise or sofa—so we can both relax without you having to sit at your desk. It's wonderful to have a place we can be together without being in your aunt's rooms all the time."

Alvin took my hand into both of his. "It's our home too, Deb."

"I'll never be comfortable downstairs, but I'll do my best to feel at home within our rooms." I pulled out my hatpin and set it and my second-best hat on the dresser in the bedroom before closing the hall door against the atmosphere of the house. "Your aunt doesn't like me."

"She's been nothing but inviting. You overthink things."

I hurried back to the sitting room and closed that hall door before responding from the threshold between the two rooms. "I sense things, and that woman is decidedly disgruntled in her so-called 'two-for-one' situation. I'm extra baggage. I wouldn't be surprised if she tried to get rid of me at the earliest opportunity."

"Let's have none of your fancies." He took me in his arms and kissed my forehead. "You wanted to be part of my Mobile adventure, and I'll not have you despairing now that we're here. We have each other, Deb. You swore to me that was enough."

"And it is, Alvin. I'm just excitable from the train ride and lack of sleep. I'll settle down in no time." My arms went over his shoulders, and I drew his head down so I could kiss his lips. I would play the part of his dutiful wife but would forever be watching my back where Aunt Catherine was concerned.

Two

That evening, Alvin and I washed and dressed for supper, returning to the parlor a few minutes before seven. Catherine looked me over from my high lace collar to the modest heeled shoes on my feet as she fingered the scooped neckline of her own rose-colored evening gown.

"Really, Alvin, you should see that Deborah dresses with a bit more care. Gray never flatters a young woman."

"Deborah dresses herself according to her own wishes, Aunt Catherine."

"No, no, Alvin. I'm Cathy, remember?" She approached where he stood beside my chair and fingered the round Alabama Polytechnic Institute seal pin he always wore on the lapel of his suit. "A man like you deserves a woman in top form beside him."

His cheeks colored. "There's nothing wrong with Deborah's form. She always looks beautiful, but we aren't accustomed to fancy suppers."

"But tonight is a celebration! A party to mark your arrival." Her eyes flashed condescendingly toward me.

"I'm sorry to disappoint you." Alvin shuffled sideways until he had more breathing space between him and his aunt. "We weren't informed you planned anything extra. Should we change into our wedding clothes?"

"It's too late for that. Besides, I'm festive enough for all of us, aren't I?" She swung her hips and angled her bosom toward him saucily.

"Of course, Cathy." He looked at me, taking my hand in his warm one. "You're wonderful too."

A moment later, the pocket doors opened between the parlor and the dining room.

"Supper, ma'am." The cook, a freckled young woman, glanced at us with light blue eyes, curtsied to the lady of the house, and made a hasty exit as though afraid to stay.

"That's a different helper than the one you had at Easter," Alvin remarked.

"Yes, that's Tessa. She's here for dinner and supper daily. We see to our own breakfast. The old cook turned useless after Jerald's death. I tend to think she felt it was her cooking that did him in, though I don't see how that's possible since I always ate the same thing he did—just in smaller amounts." Catherine attached herself to Alvin's arm. "I couldn't tolerate her weepy eyes and the memories they evoked. You understand, don't you?"

"Yes, Cathy. Uncle Jerald was a fine man." Alvin went for the dining table with her.

"You're so understanding." She leaned into his six-foot frame in a much too familiar way before taking the seat he pulled out for her at the head of the table.

Alvin escorted me to the chair on the side closest the parlor before taking the spot across from me. I smiled at him, and he winked in return.

Catherine snapped her napkin opened and draped it on her lap.

As soon as the cook carried in the first tray, Catherine was at her. "Tessa, Alvin is to be seated at the head of the table opposite me. Bring a fresh place setting, please."

"No, Cathy, that isn't necessary. I'm already settled and more than pleased to sit across from Deborah."

Catherine frowned and shifted her shoulders, causing her rose gown to shimmer under the chandelier. "You're the man of the house and we need to respect your position. I insist on the new placement beginning tomorrow at Sunday dinner."

Tessa nodded before hurrying back to the kitchen for her next load.

After seeing her close-up, the images and words connected with Tessa were brighter in my head.

Trapped.

Blackmail.

She wasn't timid; she was frightened of her employer. She was typically brash, but Catherine put fear into her when she took the position, wielding her power like a noose.

"Don't forget the wine, Tessa. I hope it's properly chilled." Catherine looked at Alvin. "It's for our celebration. I missed the wedding because of the short notice, but I must toast you."

Knowing this would be my final time to enjoy the view of Alvin while taking supper, I studied his precise movements and quirky mannerisms. He buttered his roll and let it sit until he was halfway through the meal, allowing time for the butter to soften into the surface appropriately. He preferred the bread warm to accomplish this easier, but he was patient.

Once the wine was poured, Catherine raised her glass. "To Alvin Farley, may he have a wonderful new beginning in this chapter of his life."

She wanted to toast him, but not *us*. I took a sip of the port, trying not to wince at the edge of sourness to it. Perhaps it was from the words, not the drink.

As soon as Alvin lowered his glass, he raised it once more and held my gaze. "And to my lovely bride. I'm blessed you're with me through the transition, Deborah."

The wine tasted better that time—especially accompanied by the look of disgust on our hostess's face.

The main portion of the meal was good, but the chocolate cake left much to be desired. Fortunately, Alvin understood my silent plea for escape as soon as he took his last bite.

"Thank you, Cathy, for a wonderful welcome, but we've had a long day with the traveling. I should see Deborah to bed."

"Do you still keep nursery hours, Deborah? You're so young."

"No, Aunt Catherine," I said as Alvin gently took my elbow after I stood. "It's nothing to do with my age. We're newlyweds and prefer to be alone after supper."

"Excuse us, Cathy," Alvin offered in apology to his glaring aunt. "We'll see you in the morning, and I'm sure we will sit up later with you tomorrow."

Once we were in our bedroom with the doors closed, Alvin shook his head. "I don't know what to say when you talk like that."

"Then kiss me," I smiled.

"Your father warned me you had a mind of your own and would do your own thing, no matter what I suggest."

"You wouldn't like me half as well if I were shy."

His lips pressed into a thin line before he spoke with the hint of a smile. "I do admire your pluck, Deb."

He leaned in for a kiss. My arms went around his shoulders. After a tantalizing connection, Alvin hugged me tight and nestled toward my ear beneath my tumbled hair.

"May I hold you all night, Deb?"

I nodded and reveled in the security of his embrace.

***

Deciding it was better to ask forgiveness than permission, I woke before the sun, carefully slipped out of Alvin's arms, and pulled on a simple green cotton dress. With my face washed and hair braided, I snuck downstairs. My bare feet were silent on the wood stairwell. On the landing before the stained-glass, I went to the left, utilizing the partial flight of servants' stairs that led directly into the kitchen.

After a speedy inventory of the ingredients available to me, I planned a breakfast menu and set to work. While the biscuits were in the oven, I whipped up a batch of honey butter and then scrambled a few eggs.

Tray laden with breakfast, I carried it up to the dresser, closed the door, and climbed onto the bed.

"Good morning, Alvin." I watched him blink through his surprise. "I've made us breakfast. Would you like to eat in bed?"

"Deb, you dear." He sat up. "I was never one for getting crumbs in bed, but it smells wonderful. Allow me to dress and—"

"Stay in your pajamas. We'll dine at your desk before it's covered with papers."

He disappeared into the bathroom, and I opened the drapes in our sitting room. Transferring the plates, cups, and silverware to the desk took little time. When Alvin joined me, he carried the armchair to the desk, giving me a place to sit across from him. Noticing me eyeing his striped sleepwear, he blushed.

"You look handsome, Alvin. I don't get to enjoy the sight of you when we're sleeping."

He grinned. "And you're beautiful by morning light. This all looks and smells wonderful, much better than the hotel food."

"I plan to cook for us each morning."

Alvin paused buttering a biscuit. "I don't remember you asking to use the kitchen."

"Do I need to? You keep telling me this is our home, and your aunt declared you the man of the house. She can't expect you to live off of day-old bread and coffee each morning because that's what she prefers."

"True." He took a bite of the biscuit, eyes widening. "What's this butter?"

"I mixed honey into it. Do you like it?"

A veil of pink briefly covered my vision as he reached for my hand. "It's sweet, just like you."

I felt myself glow with his words and the endearing smile on his face.

"You have a sweet tooth, Alvin, and I'm happy to indulge you." I giggled, and he gave a hearty laugh.

He leaned across the desk and kissed me. "You're good for me, Deb. And to think, your old pal Frenchie wanted to bet I wouldn't last the weekend with you."

I rolled my eyes. "I always thought he was dimwitted."

"The brightest minds know opposites attract."

"I do feel a magnetic pull toward you." My toes found his bare feet under the desk.

We laughed, talked, and flirted as we ate. Radiant over Alvin's relaxed attitude, I glided downstairs with the breakfast dishes while he dressed.

"You naughty child!"

I jerked to a stop as soon as my feet reached the kitchen floor.

Catherine motioned to the used pans and things I'd neatly stacked by the sink before going upstairs. "How dare you pillage my kitchen?"

"Pillage? What a fanciful word, like I'm a mighty kitchen pirate. I rather like that idea."

I unloaded the dishes and wiped the tray before setting it back on the counter where I'd found it. Then I started the sink filling with hot water for washing. She wanted me fearful, hurt—ready to run back to my parents—but there was no way I would leave Alvin to her clutches.

Huffing out a bitter breath, she tried once more to ruffle me. "You had no right to help yourself in here without permission."

I slipped the silverware into the bottom of the sink and turned off the water. After calmly adding our plates to the basin, I turned to the red-faced woman. She looked nothing like the regal lady who had presided over supper last night. Her hair was in a plain bun and her black dress was appropriate enough to garb a pious widow attending church.

"I'm sorry you're offended, Aunt Catherine, but it was by your words that I felt welcomed to do what was needed. My Alvin, who you proclaimed the head of the household, requires a hearty breakfast. He needs something that will stick with him until he can take a lunch break."

"But it's the Sabbath, not a work day."

"A morning is a morning, and he must be fed. I took inventory of what was available and decided on the menu so as not to drain your pantry or ice box. Should I speak with the cook about adding a few additional items to your grocery orders or do you handle the accounts yourself?"

"You impertinent—"

"I'm only seeing Alvin properly tended, which you yourself have voiced concern over."

"Then I'll have Tessa arrive for breakfast duty!"

Not one to use servant's stairs, Alvin came through the far doorway in his Sunday suit and red bowtie. "No, thank you, Cathy. I want Deborah to see to my breakfast. She knows exactly what I like. You needn't bother the help over me. The extra grocery money will be enough strain on the budget as is."

Catherine's face calmed in an instant as she went for him, a hand patting his arm. "I'm only concerned with what's best for you. Surely a hired girl would do a better job."

"It wouldn't be possible." With his chin raised, he looked at me with pride. "Deborah's meal was perfection."

Grinning over our victory, I turned to the sink and started washing the dishes. Alvin might not realize we were at war, but I was pleased he was standing up for me.

"In fact," Alvin continued, "I'd like Deborah to do all the baking for the household. Her cakes and breads are delicious, as are everything else she creates. And she even cleans up after herself."

"I can see that." The defeat in Catherine's voice was short-lived. "And I noticed she isn't dressed for church. Will you escort me to services, Alvin?"

I scrubbed the plate roughly, hoping Alvin would keep our bond strong.

"Not today, Cathy. I'd like to finish settling in, then take Deborah around town this afternoon and tomorrow as I'll be working Tuesday. Labor Day should be a good time for her to learn her way around."

"Of course. Let me know if I can be of assistance."

Her forced politeness as she exited sent currents through the room. As soon as they rippled away, I turned to my husband.

"Thank you for defending me against the tyrant."

"Oh, Deb." Alvin kissed my cheek. "Control your wild imaginings. They'll get you in trouble one day."

Hugging him, I nestled against his suit jacket. "Not with you around."

Three

Once Alvin's books were arranged on the shelves and his desk set in order, he caught my gaze where I sat in the chair by the window. After unpacking all our clothing, I had settled my sewing basket beside my proclaimed spot.

"Will you be happy here, Deb?"

"Home is wherever you are, Alvin."

"Shall we walk to the park after our noon dinner? There's one a few blocks east."

"That would be nice, especially if it's just the two of us."

The dinner bell rang downstairs, barely penetrating the oasis of our closed room.

"Time to go to the guillotine," I remarked.

"That's hardly fair," Alvin said.

"She called me a naughty child and told me I had pillaged her kitchen."

"You do have a naughty side." He laughed with a twinkle in his eyes that caused me to giggle.

We went hand-in-hand to the dining room. Seeing my lonely chair in the middle of the long side of the table brought my gaiety to a halt. Catherine hadn't arrived, so I shifted my place setting toward Alvin's end to be easily within touching distance.

Once I was seated, Alvin kissed my forehead. "I admire the way you think, Deb, but I fear you make things difficult for yourself."

"Being close to you is worth any discomfort that might be thrown my way."

Catherine found us seated together, holding hands. Her venomous gaze was directed solely at me, but Alvin saw it for the first time.

"Cathy," he said as he stood to escort her to her seat, "what has you so upset?"

"I don't know what you see in such a contrary young sprite. Deborah is completely at odds with me, and I've done nothing to merit her rebelliousness." She sniffed back a tear as Alvin handed her his handkerchief.

"Deborah isn't a child. She's a young woman—an adult like us."

"She's nothing like us. She flaunts her relationship with you, reminding me that I'm alone in this world."

"I'm doing nothing but living my life the best way I possibly can," I said. "I'm sorry if you feel it's an attack, but it isn't meant as one."

"Is it the placement of the chair?" Alvin asked with his soothing voice.

She nodded, still sniffing. "Among other things."

"Deb, perhaps if you returned the place setting—"

"I will not." I stood, controlling the anger that threatened to boil over. "Alvin, I won't bridle my enthusiasm for our life together. And Aunt Catherine, if a woman of your apparent worldliness didn't realize what company a newlywed couple would

be, that isn't something to blame on me. I already apologized
though I meant no ill. If anything, you could show understanding
to those in a new situation, away from friends and parents, and in
a strange city. It might take your mind off your own pains to lift
the burden of another."

Alvin's square jaw shifted as though he were grinding his
teeth.

"Please excuse me," I said, "but I've lost my appetite."

Alvin met me in the parlor, a hand on my arm.
"Deborah," he whispered, "you can't walk out."

"If I don't, I'll say something unforgivable." I kissed the
corner of his mouth. "You know where to find me after you eat."

I went up the stairs, collected my straw hat, and exited the
front door with a soft click.

Alvin had mentioned the park was east, so I turned that
way on Palmetto Street. Several people waved from their porches
as I passed, many with questioning eyes as they took in the
appearance of a stranger in their neighborhood.

Four blocks away, I found the public square. Grass, oak
trees, a plethora of dormant azalea bushes, iron benches, and a
deer statue decorated the park that sat as an island between the
streets. I walked the perimeter, glancing at those promenading in
their ruffled dresses and ignoring the squeals of joyful children. I
took an empty bench near where I started. Heaviness filled my
soul at the thought that I was neither a mature woman nor a
playful child. Catherine was probably right in treating me like a
girl. I didn't know enough to dress properly for the situation—in
this case, a Sunday walk—nor was I mature enough to set aside
my excitement for my husband.

Squeezing my eyes closed, I willed the tears away as I took
several deep breaths while fiddling with my pearl earrings.
Thoughts of Alvin chased the darkness from my soul. If someone
as wholesome as him could love me, then there was good inside
me, even if I kept secrets from him.

"Come on, Drew, don't drag your feet."

The words were ordinary, but the golden tone captured my attention in an instant. Opening my eyes, I focused on the threesome strolling up the sidewalk.

"I know you can keep up with your sister better than that."

It was the man speaking to the younger child, trying to sound gruff but his cheerfulness burbled with warmth—something I could imagine Alvin doing. The bright aura glowing from him was in direct opposition to the two dark shadows hovering over his shoulders.

"But I wanna play ball," the boy whined.

"You know your mother won't allow that on Sunday."

"Then can I go play tag with Jacob and the others?" He motioned to the street on the far side of the park, but I was focused on the shapes around the man in an attempt to discern their true forms.

He ruffled the boy's brown hair, similar to his own. "Go on, Drew. We'll wait for you here."

The girl looked about twelve—stick-straight but leggy in her black tights beneath the blue dress that barely covered her knees. She sat beside the man on the bench diagonally across from me and pushed the wire-rimmed glasses up her nose.

He leaned toward her with his full attention. "Now, Ethelwynne, tell me how you're feeling about the new school year."

Her voice was too soft for me to make out, but the body language between them was easy. They were comfortable together. Trusting. Then why the spirits at his back? They were too far away for me to hear any messages, but they couldn't be protecting the girl from him, for there was clearly no malice. He was possibly the children's older brother or father. Maybe an uncle.

"How other children treat you has no bearing on your worth," he said with conviction. "Students are often too dense at this age to see the true potential in each other. You'll have no problems once you come of age, darling. Your intelligence and beauty will shine through even stronger. These awkward years are but a moment in your lifetime though they seem forever when you're living it."

She nodded, braids slipping over her shoulders as she hunched on the bench.

He put his arm around her and quickly kissed her forehead. "Trust me, Ethelwynne, and talk with me whenever you need to. If you'd rather go read, I understand. I'll wait for Drew."

She hugged him, then ran across Chatham Street and slipped through the gate across from the park.

As soon as she was safely inside the yard, the man met my gaze and deliberately crossed the walkway towards me. He cut a fine figure in his three-piece suit—but not as pleasing as Alvin. When he was within four feet, the shadows behind him quivered, briefly taking the forms of two young women before fading once more.

"Good afternoon," he said. "I couldn't help but notice you seemed overly interested in my dealings."

I smiled, head angling to the side to try a different perspective.

Dreams.

Second sight.

Love!

The words discharged in my mind like cheap firecrackers, causing me to physically flinch.

"Are you all right, miss?" He went to touch my left hand that had flailed against the arm of the bench. "I beg your pardon, missus. You look so young, I didn't think."

I fingered my ring and laughed, pleased to have been acknowledged as a married woman by a stranger for the first time. "I was married on Friday."

He grinned, showcasing a chipped front tooth. "Well, congratulations on your nuptials. But do you feel unwell? Should I collect the lucky man to assist you?"

"I'm fine, thank you."

"I'm sorry, but I don't recognize you, though I feel as if I should know you."

"You're very perceptive. Is that from your second sight?"

He blanched, his smile fading as his golden brown eyes took on a haunted cast. "How did you know?"

"I have a gift myself, though it doesn't come in dreams."

The dimples on his cheeks were back along with his grin. "You do know! Tell me more."

"Maybe you should sit down."

One of the shadows stayed with him, but the other floated in front of me, seeming to put a hand on a hip.

"My name is Deborah Farley. I arrived yesterday with my husband, Alvin. We're from the Montgomery area, but Alvin grew up in Birmingham."

"Welcome to Mobile, Mrs. Farley." He offered his hand. "I'm Sean Francis Spunner. I've been in this neighborhood over half my life, and down near the river for the first twelve years."

His handshake was firm and friendly.

Too friendly.

A blast of chill air swept over me as though the shadow tried to shove me.

"You have two very protective spirits with you, Mr. Spunner."

"Is that what drew your attention?"

I liked that he didn't question my word. "It was your voice. My eyes were closed, and I heard you speak to the boy. Is he your son, the girl your daughter or niece?"

"No, but I claim them as kin. I'm good friends with their parents. They live across the street, but you know that as you watched Ethelwynne leave."

I nodded. "You have a wonderful way with them. Is there any connection between them and the two young women with you? The figures don't appear to be together, but they both claim you."

"It must be my two lost loves." He features softened with loss. "But why not my parents?"

I touched his hand. "I'm sorry, Mr. Spunner. Please know that your parents love you as well, but this one…she's possessive of you. She doesn't like us touching, no matter how innocent."

"My Eliza." He bit his lip and looked heavenward. "She claimed me like I'd never thought possible. We were to be married, but she had an accident—an accident I'd dreamt about and tried to prevent."

"It wasn't your fault." I removed my hand from his. "She understands you tried. They both do. They mean you no ill. They're here for love and…and one of them also…"

The cold air was back despite it being close to ninety degrees, then retreated.

"She closed herself off."

"How?" Mr. Spunner asked.

"She moved to the bench you previously sat on." Images of two people entangled in the night flashed through my mind. "Did you neck there with her at some point?"

His laugh turned several heads our way. "A time or two, yes. I still miss her touch."

"How long has it been?"

"Five years this next January." He shook his head. "I need to let her go, but I haven't been able to shake her from my mind."

"Because she's clinging to you, Mr. Spunner." I paused. How would I react if I was forced away from Alvin because of death? I would probably want to stay with him as well. "What about the other one? She's quiet, her hold more of curiosity than control. I don't think she's always with you. Maybe when you're near something connected to her."

"Winifred, my first love." He motioned to the gate the girl had gone through. "Winnie died in that house thirteen years ago. Ethelwynne is her cousin's daughter. I often feel close to Winnie when I visit them."

"She's pleased that you love her extended family."

"Is she speaking to you?"

"Not in the way you might expect. I hear words or see images. Nothing more than quick glimpses. I don't typically see the spirits communicating with me, but these two are very active this afternoon, almost like they're fighting over you."

Mr. Spunner laughed. "It was almost like two lifetimes to me—before Winnie's death and after. I grew up that summer in more ways than one."

I was silent as his thoughts caressed his mind, allowing him to recall the beauty before the sadness.

He met my gaze once more. "There's something sinister about all this. Not you, Miss Deborah, but the situation. I'm glad Winnie isn't chained to me. Could you help free Eliza?"

"I've never attempted something like that, but I could try. Not here, but some other time."

"Of course."

The sensation that I was being watched prickled my spine. Looking back at Palmetto Street, I saw Alvin at the corner.

"My husband is coming," I said hurriedly. "Please don't—he doesn't know about this."

"But why, when it's such a part of you?"

"He wouldn't understand. Not fully anyway. But he knows there's something different about me." I blushed, realizing how it must look that I showed my true self to a stranger when my husband wasn't aware.

"Deborah, I'm glad you're here." Alvin's gaze went from me to the stranger on the bench I was sitting with.

Mr. Spunner went to his feet. "Allow me to introduce myself, Mr. Farley. I'm Sean Spunner. I happened across your wife a short time ago, and we've been chatting while I wait for a youngster to finish his games. Congratulations on your wedding and earning such a prize as this intelligent young woman. May your days together be blessed."

"Thank you. I'm fond of Deborah and have been worried about her this hour as we parted under a less than ideal situation."

Mr. Spunner's eyes narrowed and he straightened his posture as though ready to defend me.

"It wasn't Alvin's fault," I said.

"Nor was it completely Deborah's," Alvin added.

Which meant he did blame me a little.

"We moved in with my widowed aunt on Rapier," Alvin began to explain.

"I'm at Rapier and Palmetto," Mr. Spunner said. "You must come to supper sometime. Althea does wonders with food."

"Is that your wife?" Alvin asked.

"My cook."

"He lost his fiancée," I said in a tone just above a whisper, knowing her spirit still watched.

"How unfortunate for you, Mr. Spunner," Alvin said.

"Do call me Sean, the both of you." He thumped Alvin's upper arm with a light punch. "You're a solid chap. What do you do?"

"My specialty is geometry, but I teach any mathematics. I've been hired at Barton Academy. I taught last year at the school Deb's father is principal of. And please, call us Alvin and Deborah as well."

I fingered Alvin's A.P.I. pin on his suit lapel. "Alvin played fullback in college."

"Some of the guys from my gym get together for games on a couple Saturdays in the autumn, and I'm one of the team captains this year. I'll keep you informed, if you're interested."

"I'd enjoy that. Thank you." Alvin tucked my arm through his. "Now, Deb, how about that stroll we wanted?"

I motioned to my simple dress and scoffed. "I'm all wrong Alvin. I didn't think about it being Sunday when I dressed. I look a fright compared to all the people around us, including you."

"Nonsense, Deborah. You're respectfully clothed."

"Yes, for a country walk or picnic, not a Sunday stroll through town."

"If I may be so bold," Sean said, "I proclaim your husband sensible in his declaration. The beauty of simplicity is often lost these days, but if it would help you feel more comfortable, I would walk with you on your other side."

"But what of the boy you're watching?"

He glanced at his pocket watch. "His mother will be calling for him soon. I'll send him home and be happy to show the two of you around. We could even drive downtown in my automobile, if you'd like."

Smiling at the idea of a private tour of the city, I looked to my husband. "Could we?"

Alvin nodded at me before looking at our new friend. "Thank you, Sean. We gladly accept your offer."

Four

The next morning, I lay beside Alvin, waiting for him to wake. I thought of our previous afternoon with Sean Spunner. He proved to be a wonderful tour guide, full of information about everything from architecture to scandalous stories of politicians and Mardi Gras societies. Maybe it was his tragic losses that humbled him, or the connection we shared over his spirit visitors, but Sean was beyond friendly for a mature bachelor of thirty—five years Alvin's senior.

Bored with waiting, I snuggled against Alvin and hoped my roaming touch would rouse him.

"Morning, Deb," he muttered as he captured my hand off his abdomen and brought it to his lips.

"Do you wish more sleep, or will you keep me company while I cook?"

"What about a third option?"

"What's that?"

Alvin pulled me to him. "Stay in bed with me."

I met his lips, pleased he was initiating something out of the ordinary. I was more than willing to indulge him, but his stomach gave a rumbling growl.

After a deep kiss, I sat up. "Breakfast it is."

He rubbed his belly. "It's never done that this early before."

"It must have been all that energy you used last night." I giggled and went for the closet.

He watched every move I made when I turned for the dresser with my outfit.

"You bring me to life, Deb."

I tossed fresh undergarments over my shoulder and smiled. "And you awaken my heart."

Bacon was frying and pancakes were cooking when Alvin wrapped me in his arms from behind. Kissing my ear, he trailed a hand down the side of my apron. I turned in his embrace and kissed him with nibbling affection.

"You taste good," he murmured, "but don't burn the bacon. I like the taste of that, too."

"And maple syrup?" I asked as I flipped the strips and hotcakes in the two pans on the stovetop.

"Whatever you serve, it won't be as sweet as you." He pulled me into his arms once more, caressing hands roaming over the backside of my navy skirt as his searching kiss claimed my mouth. My arms went around his shoulders, my sky blue shirtwaist against his white button-down and blue bowtie.

I heard the creak of the floorboard in the hall, but didn't pull away. Aunt Catherine was welcome to see how much we loved each other. Maybe it would help her accept me as Alvin's wife.

Alvin soon held a platter while I loaded it with pancakes and bacon. He watched me pour more batter into the hot pan for the next batch.

"You have a steady hand, Deb. They're all congruent."

I smiled. "Coffee or tea?"

"Always coffee in the mornings."

A few minutes later, he carried our place settings to the dining room while I finished the food.

"What a surprise, Cathy. I didn't expect to see you up this early." Alvin's voice carried from the next room.

"Do you think someone can sleep through the smell of cooking bacon?"

He laughed. "There's plenty. Will you join us?"

"If it wouldn't be an inconvenience."

"Of course not."

When Alvin returned to the kitchen, I had another place setting ready, plus a frown to go with it.

"Don't be sour, Deb." He kissed my nose. "Your breakfast smells amazing to everyone."

I tried to keep a straight face.

"There's that's teasing curl of your lips, like a fern frond unfurling."

The wording was awkward but romantic because it was completely Alvin. I laughed and hugged him before he returned to the dining room to finish setting the table.

When I carried in the platter of food, Catherine had him cornered by the window. She was in a silk dressing gown and wrap, the opening of it shockingly low on her ample bosom.

"It's marvelous to see you without your suit jacket on, Alvin. Do relax more around the house. It is your home, after all."

I set the food down and turned back to the kitchen without word. Returning with the coffee, I caught Alvin's eye and forced a smile.

"Do you need help with anything else?" he asked.

"No, it's all ready."

"I hope you don't mind me joining you," Catherine said as she strolled to her chair. "Alvin wanted to share with me."

"It's no trouble, and good morning, Aunt Catherine."

"Cathy, dear. You keep forgetting."

I smiled sweetly and passed her the platter. "I haven't forgotten that I must treat my elders with respect and that includes using proper titles."

Danger.

The word came to me a split second before hatred burned in her eyes. I immediately turned to Alvin, but he was looking at his plate as he cut a neat wedge from his stack of pancakes. I wasn't sure if he was ignoring my pointed remark or too enraptured with his breakfast to have noticed the exchange between his aunt and me.

We ate in silence several minutes.

"What are your plans for the holiday, Alvin?" Catherine asked.

"Deborah and I are going to walk to Barton Academy this morning to time how long it will take me to get to work."

"Won't she slow you down?"

"Deborah has always kept up with me."

"Isn't the gentleman supposed to match his pace with the lady? But I suppose she's used to running about."

While washing the breakfast dishes, I felt Catherine's vile presence enter the kitchen. She stopped close enough to touch me and whispered, her bitter coffee breath heating my neck.

"Please realize your games are doing nothing but chasing Alvin into my arms. I was so upset after you walked out yesterday he had to hold me as I cried. His shoulder in an excellent pillow for a grieving widow."

She aimed to invoke anger. I gave her no attention, let alone an emotional response.

I rinsed another plate and set it on a clean towel to dry later.

"I thought you were all about manners and respecting your elders, yet you ignore me."

After placing the next plate on the clean pile, I spoke without turning around, though I watched her reflection in the window over the sink. "My mother taught me if I can't say anything nice, I shouldn't speak. I'm sure what I'd say about you would not be considered nice, Aunt Catherine, so please excuse my silence."

With a muttered, unladylike curse, she left the kitchen.

Half an hour later, I strolled down the sidewalk on Alvin's arm. He had checked his pocket watch before he opened the front door.

I knew his brain was taking in everything as we headed toward Government Street, so I happily walked beside him without speaking.

"It's a wonderful neighborhood, isn't it?" He squeezed my hand. "Just the place to raise a family."

"We will populate Mobile with little Farleys in no time."

He laughed, but when we reached the main road, he stopped and turned to me. "I know our living arrangement isn't ideal, but I'm pleased you're here with me. And I'm not just saying that because I've eaten the best breakfasts I've ever had in my life the past two days in a row."

"I know. You like the nights as well." I grinned up at him.

Alvin tilted his head and shrugged, trying to suppress a smile.

"Come on." I kissed his cheek. "I don't want us to throw off your timing. I'd hate to think you'll stop on a corner to sweet talk a girl on the way to work every day."

He grinned. "Not unless it's you, Deb."

The columned, three-story building and its soaring rotunda on the north side of Government Street greeted us over a dozen blocks later.

"Twenty-four minutes," Alvin declared after checking the time. "Rain might slow me down, but I could hop on a streetcar those days. Maybe a new bicycle would be a good investment since I sold my old one before the move."

The school property was locked for the holiday, but we surveyed the exterior from outside the gate. A few shadows loomed in the upper windows, causing me to fear for Alvin. Something wasn't right within the walls, but there was no time to dwell on it.

We left Barton Academy and explored the business district that Sean had driven us through the day before. Many shops were closed, and the Labor Day parade was already finished, but the crowds remained, strolling the streets and filling the benches in the public areas. We were just another couple in the crowd, enjoying a day off in the city. Even with the fleeting messages from beyond that came and went like birds playing chase in an orchard, I was completely at peace.

"Let's go in that cathedral Sean pointed out yesterday," Alvin said. "I see the spires on the next block."

He had wanted to stop in with Sean yesterday, but I'd refused on the grounds I wasn't dressed nice enough. I tightened my hold on Alvin's hand. He squeezed it lovingly in return and hurried his steps.

"See the symmetry in the window placements, Deb?" He asked as we entered the side gate. "And those giant columns on the portico. The inside must be fascinating."

I grew dizzy from the assault of emotions pouring from the structure as we climbed the front steps.

Love.

Faith.

Loss.

Just before he led us through a door, a mustached man exited it. He paused and looked us over before turning to Alvin. "Her head, sir. It must be covered before entering the sanctuary."

"Oh, we didn't know. I beg your pardon," Alvin replied.

The sudden stop whirled my pulsing senses, but I managed to smile. "Go on, Alvin, I'll wait here."

Alvin entered without pause. I went to one of the massive columns in the center of the portico and leaned a hand on it as another wave of feelings threatened to drown me.

Death.

Horrors.

Disease.

"If you want to go in, miss," the man said, "some ladies use a handkerchief when they don't have a proper mantilla with them. I have a clean one I'd gladly give you."

"No, but thank you," I said with a quiver in my voice. "I'll wait here."

"Are you all right?" He came closer. "It looks like your strength is draining before my eyes."

"It's been a long walk, but I'm fine." I closed my eyes, further leaning into the fluted column.

"Should I fetch your gentleman?"

"I don't wish to intrude on his adventure." I forced myself to look alert. "But have you happened to see Mr. Spunner about? Sean Spunner."

"Spunner, sure. He always comes to morning Mass on holidays. He left not too long ago." The man stepped to the edge of the portico and called to someone passing on the sidewalk. "Mr. Brady! Have you seen Spunner?"

The younger man came to the front gate, smoothing his sideburns. "He was in Bienville Square a minute ago."

"Run get him, please. Tell him it's dire."

The man on the sidewalk looked at me and then ran off as the mustached man returned to my side.

"You didn't need to do that," I said.

"Nonsense." He offered his arm. "Come sit on the north steps in the shade. I'm Maxwell Easton, by the way. How do you know Sean?"

"We're neighbors. My husband and I met him in Washington Square yesterday afternoon, and he drove us around town. Alvin—my husband—and I are seeing things on foot today."

Mr. Easton laughed. "And here I was thinking I was sending for Spunner to help a pretty damsel in distress, but you're already spoken for."

"I hope he won't be upset by you calling him here."

"Spunner is amiable and it will be no drain on the younger fellow who ran for him. He's one of his boxing friends." He helped me lower to the steps. "You sure don't look well, missus…"

"Deborah Farley, formerly of Montgomery County."

"Well, Mrs. Farley, I'm sure Spunner will be here in a jiffy. Your husband, on the other hand, looked awed when he entered the cathedral. I'm not sure how long he'll be."

"We've never been inside a Catholic church before. There aren't many up north."

Sean and the messenger ran in the gate, though a shadow stayed on the sidewalk.

"Deborah!" Sean knelt beside me. "What's wrong? Where's Alvin?"

"Alvin is inside. I wanted to go with him, but I—I got overwhelmed. Mr. Easton insisted on calling for you."

"Max has known me since I was a runty kid trying to look up his sisters' skirts."

All the men laughed, including the younger fellow who had fetched Sean. He appeared to be about my age.

Seeing that I looked to him, he smiled.

Sean turned to him and stood. "Thanks for your assistance, Chuck. We appreciate it, but you aren't needed any more."

Mr. Easton grinned. "Yes, and don't be jealous of Spunner. Mrs. Farley is married."

Chuck Brady fingered his long sideburns and stepped back. "Well, I'm happy to be of service at any rate. Enjoy your holiday."

As he walked away, Sean turned to Mr. Easton. "Thank you for getting me. I've got things from here, Max. Your family is waiting for you."

"Has Lottie made it to Bienville Square with the children?"

"She has and she looks tuckered out. Make sure she gets a rest today."

"I will." He shook Sean's hand and looked down at me. "It was lovely to meet you, Mrs. Farley. I hope your strength returns."

"Thank you, Mr. Easton."

As soon as he was through the gate, I caught Sean's eye as tears flooded mine. "Is there a graveyard nearby?"

"Good Lord, you are sensitive!" He handed me a silk handkerchief from his suit pocket. "We're sitting on it. The graves were moved to make room for the cathedral and everything across from us when it was built last century. There are rumors of bones still being here, but no one knows for sure."

"They're here, Sean. So many." A tear streaked down my cheek. "All those souls, coupled with the despair of the mourners from the countless funerals held here makes this a very sad place."

"But what of the weddings and baptisms?" His voice rose with the question. "The cathedral is a place of joy."

"I didn't mean to give offensive, but the sadness is louder. So many feel alone."

"And Eliza?" he whispered. "Her funeral was across the bay, but we were to be married here."

"Eliza is guarded. She stopped at the gate when she saw me."

His dimples winked as he grinned. "Keeping secrets means a lot to a minx like her. I didn't know half of what went on in her mind, but that kept things exciting for me."

I closed my eyes, trying to focus on the love pouring from him at the memory of his beloved rather than the despair that permeated the location.

"Deborah, are you all right?"

"I will be."

"Shall I take you away from here?"

"No, thank you. I have to wait for Alvin."

"Should I get him?"

I shook my head. "He's enjoying himself. He has to be or he would have returned by now."

"Then I'll wait with you." He clasped his hands in his lap. "Would talking ease your emotions or make it worse?"

"You have a soothing nature when you speak."

"It comes in handy when I try to charm the jury." His tone was light, but I felt the heaviness about him he was trying to dispel. "Are you fond of books?"

"I prefer to listen to people read, because I'd rather be doing something with my hands. I love to cook and bake as well as knit and sew. Alvin will never go hungry or have a hole in his sock."

"He's a blessed man." Our gazes locked and he leaned closer. "You should tell him about your gift, Deborah."

"It feels more like a curse today."

"Alvin loves you. You need to rely on him in all things."

"Deb! What's going on?" Alvin hurried down the steps so he could come around the front of me. His gaze flashed between me and Sean, his jaw tight with concern and a slight tremor of uncertainty.

"I'm all right now." I raised my hand and Alvin assisted me in standing. Leaning into him, I wished for a hug, but he was too rigid with emotions. "I grew lightheaded, and the man who was by the door when you went in sent for Sean to stay with me."

"I'm sorry I kept you out here in the heat. It's very cool inside, and I lost all track of time." He briefly cupped my cheek as he studied my face. "You do look pale. Let's get home."

"Allow me to drive you," Sean said as he stood. "I insist."

At the cathedral gate, the young man who fetched Sean waited for us.

"The mysterious husband!" he said with an urbane smile. "I thought Mr. Easton made that up to clear me out."

Sean laughed. "Chuck Brady, meet Alvin and Deborah Farley, two of my newest neighbors. Alvin begins teaching at Barton Academy this month. Alvin and Deborah, Chuck works at Gayfer's Department Store and is a regular at the gym I use."

As Alvin and Chuck shook hands, the young man zeroed in on Alvin's Alabama Polytechnic Institute pin and his eyes sparked. "Did you happen to play any sports in school?"

Alvin nodded. "Football, all through high school and college."

"Football on a Southern Intercollegiate team! What position?"

"Fullback." Alvin grinned.

Chuck playfully punched Alvin's solid middle. "And what are you, two hundred?"

"And a nickel." Alvin grinned.

"You're just what we need, Mr. Farley. On the steps of the cathedral, a miracle has occurred! Do you see the size of his neck, Spunner?"

"Of course I did." Sean smirked at him. "I recruited Alvin yesterday. He'll be on my team."

"Then, by God, so am I! We've never had someone who's played above high school level, and Davenport is out this year. He says it's too stressful on his wife because she's in the family way, but I think that's an excuse because he's getting too old."

"I've got two years on him, but we'll talk about it later," Sean said. "I'm going to drive the Farleys home."

More hands were shaken, and then I was whisked away. Once seated beside Alvin on the plump leather seat, I rested against his shoulder. I tried not to think of him holding Aunt Catherine as he put his arm around me.

"Do you forgive me, Deb?" he whispered.

"There's nothing to forgive, Alvin. I told you to go in the church without me."

I snuggled under his arm, not caring about the heat. Feeling his security was all I needed.

Sean pulled to a stop in front of the house and turned to us. "You're welcome to come over anytime, the both of you. I'm just across the next intersection—the corner house. I have an extensive library, and you may borrow any books you want. If I'm not home but Althea is there, she'll give you entrance. Don't be shy."

We thanked him and went inside.

Alvin insisted on my drinking a glass of iced tea and then brought me upstairs to rest. I didn't see Catherine, but I felt her lying in wait.

Five

I awoke alone and disoriented.

The exhaustion I'd experienced from the emotions at the cathedral was no longer, but my mind felt uneasy. Or maybe it was my soul.

Deceit.

I slipped off the bed and slowly opened the door. Not pausing to put on my shoes, I stopped at the top of the stairs, dizzy with the height as I looked down at the stained glass on the landing.

"Are you sure you want to wake her for supper?" Catherine asked from somewhere below.

"She didn't eat dinner," Alvin replied.

"But we could dine together again—the two of us." Her voice sought to caress. "We could sit close, like you prefer, and have a proper conversation."

"I don't want Deborah to wake in the night hungry. She might be restless."

"And that would disturb your sleep." She paused. "There is the other bedroom next to mine. Or the sleeping balcony off of my room. You're always welcome to either, Alvin. We can't allow that child to spoil your first week of work."

Not wanting the vulture to tear Alvin from me, I went back for my low-heeled slippers and pranced down the stairs as noisily as I could.

Alvin was standing beside Catherine, who sat on the little sofa. I had no doubt he had been sitting close with her, too afraid to move lest he give offense.

"I'm sorry for sleeping all afternoon," I said.

He met me in the open space of the hall outside the parlor and took my hand. "You needed it, Deborah. I'm glad to see you looking well. I've kept you too busy the past few days with traveling and exploring our new city."

"I've enjoyed every moment with you." I kissed his cheek and smiled.

"I didn't want to dine without you." He brought me to the large sofa, and we sat side-by-side, still holding hands.

My smile was probably triumphant, but I didn't hide it from the woman across the room. I did guard my tongue at the supper table because the contention the day before had affected Alvin's peace.

After supper, I sat silently for an hour in the parlor knitting an intricate blue shawl while Alvin read aloud. Catherine had requested a collection of sonnets by Shakespeare, no doubt in an attempt to woo him to her with romantic thoughts, which proved how little she knew about my husband. Alvin detested the old English writers. He would have been comfortable with something more modern like Lewis Carroll or Arthur Conan Doyle—writers who knew patterns, games, and cleverness better than flowery words. The awkwardness of his voice with the sensual words solidified my love for him. I would do anything to protect him from Catherine's schemes.

The next morning, I woke from troubled dreams about Catherine, but managed to have an omelet, hot toast, and coffee ready for Alvin when he came downstairs.

Once he was eating, I questioned him from my chair at the dining table. "Would you like to bring your lunch with you, or should I deliver it?"

"I'm not sure when my break will be, so I'll bring it." He motioned to my coffee cup. "Aren't you going to eat?"

"I will after I see you off."

Catherine left us blessedly alone, but she appeared as soon as I waved goodbye to Alvin from the front porch.

"And what will you do with yourself all day, Deborah?" she asked from the bottom of the stairs when the front door closed behind me.

"First, I'll see to my own breakfast—and yours as well, if you would like—and then I'll bake our dessert so I'm not in Tessa's way when she arrives later."

She declined my breakfast offer, but took much longer than necessary when preparing her own coffee and bread with apple jelly. I ate perched on the kitchen stool, a plate on my lap. Catherine sneered at me before daintily carrying her tray to the dining room.

When she returned, it was empty-handed.

"Fetch my dishes and wash them with yours, Deborah." She didn't wait for a reply before marching off.

After the carrot cake was out of the oven, I set it on the counter to cool along with a note to Tessa explaining I would frost it before supper. I went upstairs to tidy the bedroom and wash in preparation for leaving the house.

With my hat and handbag, I headed toward the front door.

"Where do you think you're going?" Catherine said from where she lounged in the parlor.

"To the market. I need a few special ingredients for my dessert."

She eyed my simple skirt and shirtwaist. "People will mistake you for a servant."

"Like you did when you ordered me to clear your breakfast table?" I paused to enjoy the shocked expression. "I have no issues with helping, Aunt Catherine, but I'll not be ordered about by someone who is neither my employer nor parent."

"Or spouse?"

"Alvin doesn't order me to do anything."

"Well maybe he needs to."

I inclined my head. "Goodbye, Aunt Catherine."

Before I could walk the first block, an automobile pulled to the curb beside me.

Sean Spunner, an arm perched on the doorframe of his black vehicle, grinned. "Good morning, Deborah."

"Hello, Sean."

"You look like you're feeling better."

"I am, thank you."

"I'm on my way to work but would be happy to drop you wherever you need to go as my first meeting isn't until half-past the hour."

"Thank you. I need to get to a grocer or cheese shop for a few ingredients I have planned for desserts this week."

"Climb in." He got out of the car and motioned me inside.

"I do appreciate it." I slid behind the wheel and across the bench to the far window.

"Did Alvin get off to work all right?"

"He did. I'll have to think of ways to stay occupied myself. Catherine Snodgrass thinks I'm nothing more than a nursery girl invading her house. On top of that, I have a bad feeling about her. I believe Aunt Catherine would make your Eliza look like a helpless kitten."

Sean laughed. "What made you mention a kitten?"

"I heard a meow from the direction of her shadow sitting behind you."

"I called her Kitten, but she was a tigress." He pulled in front of a grocery store and winked at me. "And I loved to make her purr."

"Really, Sean!" I snatched my handbag from the seat and opened the door myself.

"I'm sorry, Deborah." He reached across and took my hand before I could stand. "I'm too free with you. You're the first person I've been able to talk to about Eliza in a long time. Althea listens, but she looks sadder every time I bring her up, especially this past year. You didn't know Eliza in life, but you know her now."

A flash of violet lit the backseat like lightning.

"She doesn't like that idea."

"Of course she doesn't." His laugh sounded choked, but he released my hand. "Please remember the offer of my library. Althea will welcome you anytime for as long as you wish. When you do stop by, let her know which day is best for you and Alvin to come for supper. She knows my schedule."

"I will, Sean. Thank you." I stood but then leaned back in. "I'm not completely scandalized. I'm a married woman after all, but talk like that would make Alvin uncomfortable. He believes intimacies should stay in the bedroom with only the couple involved."

"However did he survive years on a football team with all the guys chattering?"

"My theory is his head stayed so full of the plays that he couldn't hear anything else."

"You two are darling together—you know that, don't you?"

"I'd like to think so." I smiled at him before straightening. "Have a good day, Sean."

Half an hour later, I walked back to Rapier Avenue with my parcel of groceries. After putting the items away, complete with notes placed on them declaring my intentions, I busied myself with dusting the sitting room so Alvin's work space would be spotless on his return.

"Excuse me, ma'am."

I turned to the open door, seeing a petite young woman with round, dark eyes. She wore an apron, and a cap covered her chestnut hair, her pale hands holding a broom. No words came to me. No messages of warning or fear.

"Yes?"

"I'm here to make the beds and clean the rooms. I come every Monday through Friday except holidays."

"How nice for Aunt Catherine, but I won't need your assistance in my spaces. I'll happily see to them myself. I assume the brooms and mops are kept off the kitchen porch."

"Yes, ma'am."

"It's Mrs. Farley, but you may call me Deborah, if you'd like. What's your name?"

"Sabine, ma'am, but I couldn't call you anything except Mrs. Farley." She hurried toward Catherine's bedroom.

When I went down for noon dinner, Catherine was questioning the maid in the dining room.

"Why didn't she allow you in?"

"She said she was seeing to things herself, ma'am. The bed was made—I saw that when I peeked in earlier—and she was dusting the front room."

"Sabine is correct," I said as I took my seat without pause. "Not having been raised with a cleaning staff, I've been taught to be a competent housekeeper."

"How can you expect me to not treat you like a servant when you look and act like one?"

"Because you know better, Aunt Catherine. You're not a dimwit."

That kept her quiet throughout the meal. She looked forlorn with her sad blue eyes, so much so that I almost felt guilty for being so prickly. Alvin had told me she was lonely and he expected me to be a companion to her, but how could I be pleasant company when we were at odds all the time?

Afterward, I went to the back porch to familiarize myself with the placement of the cleaning items and then settled on the rear stoop, observing a blue jay chasing a cardinal across the narrow yard. Hemmed in by the two larger houses on either side, the small plot was half patio with the rest rose bushes surrounding a curving oyster-shell path bleached white from the sun. It was pretty, but a variety of flora would keep the space attractive in all seasons rather than the bleak space it must be in winter.

"Excuse me," Tessa said from behind the screen door.

"Sorry." I stood. "Do you need to come out?"

"No, I want to ask you about all these papers in the kitchen."

"My notes?"

She nodded as I slipped in the door.

"I thought I made myself clear on each of them."

Her shoulders hunched, and she looked at the floor.

"I'm to make dessert for supper from now on, if Catherine didn't tell you." I went into the kitchen and motioned to the two circular cakes on the plates. "Those were cooling, and the new groceries are ingredients for the frosting and other things I have planned for later this week."

"You're taking my job, too?"

"No, of course not, Tessa. Is that what you and Sabine think?"

"Mrs. Snodgrass warned us you would take over everything," she whispered.

I laughed. "I assure you I'm not. I just want control over our rooms and to prepare treats for Alvin."

"But you cook meals, too."

"I can, but only breakfast for now. I wouldn't have you or Sabine run off. Besides, it's not my place to do such things."

"But, M—"

"I'm not sure what has changed since Mr. Snodgrass's death, but I can assure you I'm trying my best *not* to ruffle the feathers with how things are currently running."

The cook's shoulders went down, the tension in her posture lessening as a blue haze surrounded her.

"I mean no harm, Tessa."

She smiled. "I know someone like you wouldn't."

Her unspoken words were that the lady of the house was another matter, but I didn't force her to say it out loud.

At four o'clock, I dressed in one of my Sunday outfits and buttoned on my good black boots so I would be presentable for supper. I hoped to be on the front porch when Alvin returned, but I was too late.

"She's a troubled girl, Alvin." Catherine's voice rose up the stairwell with its manipulating tone. "You must be firm with her. Make her know her place. It's really not fair for you to be bothered with students all day and then have to deal with an immature companion the rest of your waking hours."

"Deborah is a free spirit, Cathy. It's one of the things I love about her, but she *is* sensible and mature on many matters."

Cheeks glowing with his words, I descended the stairs. Alvin met me on the landing before the stained-glass window with a smile and offered hand for the final steps.

"I missed you today, Deb," he whispered before kissing my cheek.

It was a bold move for him, and I replied in kind with a kiss on his lips and a hug. "I missed you as well."

"Obviously not too much, Deborah," Catherine said with a snide tone as we came into the parlor. "You did, after all, get into a man's automobile this morning."

Before Alvin could think anything bad, I calmly explained. "I wouldn't say the two things are related in the slightest. I was walking to the store when Mr. Spunner passed me on his way out of the neighborhood. He dropped me at the grocer on his way to work. If there is issue with me accepting a short ride with our new friend, I'll happily decline next time, Alvin."

"Don't think such a thing, Deborah. A ride to the store is fine, especially if the weather is bad. Cathy, there's nothing to worry over. Sean is known to both of us. He's a gentleman and perfectly harmless."

"Is he?" She left her question hanging in the air with the scent of unease.

That night, when I undressed for bed, I caught Alvin watching me from the chair in the corner of our bedroom.

"I'm glad you enjoyed your day, and that you got a classroom with a view on the third floor." I opened the buttons down the front of my blue blouse. "Shall I bring your lunch to you tomorrow?"

"No thank you. There are more meetings and lesson plans for me to finish before the students arrive next week." He unbuttoned his shirt as well.

"Oh." I hung up my shirt and bolero jacket.

"Deb?"

I turned to Alvin, hands at the fastener on my waist. "Yes?"

"I like the view here even better."

He crossed the room, and I placed my arms around his shoulders. "I'm glad you do, Alvin. Would you remove my skirt for me?"

His cheeks turned rosy, but his hands trailed my waist with a sensual touch that made me quiver.

I smiled my thanks, knowing teasing words would only make him feel awkward with the task. As soon as I stepped out of it, he laid it carefully over the end of the bed. I shadowed his footsteps until he turned to me. Hands roaming under his white shirt, I declared my love for him. Alvin kissed my neck, and I swooned in his arms.

Six

On Wednesday, I left the house after the midday meal. I had a basket in my hand with a loaf of molasses bread from the double batch I'd baked that morning. Introducing myself to Althea was my goal, and I didn't want to arrive empty-handed.

Sean's home on the corner gave off a crisp, functional appeal from the sidewalk. It was a four square, similar to Catherine's, but without ornate trim or the dramatic double front door. I climbed the six steps to the porch, gazed longingly at the porch swing, and knocked.

A Black woman in a gray dress opened the door with an excess of welcoming warmth and a rich reddish-brown glow about her frame. "Come in, Mrs. Farley."

"How did you know me?"

"My boy tells me everything, and he described you to perfection, from your alabaster complexion to that button nose."

With a laugh, I stepped inside the paneled space. "Thank you, Miss Althea. Sean said I could stop by anytime."

"He surely did. I'm supposed to show you his library, but if you would like to come to the kitchen first, I have fresh oatmeal cookies and could brew some coffee right quick.

"That sounds wonderful, and I have a loaf of molasses bread for you."

Once I was settled at the small table in the cozy white and yellow kitchen with the water heating on the stove, Althea turned her large eyes on me. "Please know I don't invite all of Sean's friends into the kitchen."

"How many—a quarter of them?"

"Just one so far."

With her words, the atmosphere changed. I stayed silent until she sat across from me with coffee and cookies.

I stirred cream into my steaming cup. "What is it you want to talk to me about?"

"My boy said you were a sharp one, especially with your second sight."

I nearly choked on my coffee.

"Don't be upset, Mrs. Farley. Sean Francis tells me everything." Althea held my gaze without embarrassment.

"Call me Deborah."

"And please call me Althea. He wants you to help with Eliza, but I don't know if that's a good idea."

"Why not?" I asked.

"How can you question that when Sean Francis told me you saw her."

I smiled. "Only a glimmer, but she does seem difficult."

"You should go around the corner on Government Street and meet her mother in that mansion before agreeing to it. She's a cold one."

"Sean called Eliza a minx."

"He loved that girl, but she was a bundle of trouble. I don't see how she'll be any less now."

"I have to try, Althea. I've been seeing and feeling spirits since my great-granny passed when I was four, but I've never experienced anything like what Eliza is doing to Sean. It isn't natural. He deserves peace, and she needs rest."

"She's stubborn. I think you should first practice whatever it is you're going to do on a more willing spirit."

"I think you're giving me more credit than I deserve." I smiled nervously. "I have no idea what I'm going to do with Eliza's spirit to encourage her to leave."

"That's even more reason to practice."

"And where am I supposed to get a spare spirit?"

"The old clay pit and its ghosts are just a few blocks away."

I shook my head. "I've never gone looking, and I don't intend to now. And I'm certainly not going to barge into the location of some local folklore and mess with the energy there."

Althea laughed. "Sean said you were a firecracker. You don't look it, child, but you are."

Smiling, I stirred my coffee. "I've completely gotten under Catherine Snodgrass's skin."

"It's nothing more than she deserves. After her husband passed, she dropped both her established colored ladies and hired two young upstarts."

"Were they cheaper, a way to save her money?"

"Whites always get paid more, except those of us working for Sean Francis. My boy is the best there is." The love and respect for him in her voice spoke volumes.

"How long have you been with him?"

"Nearly half a dozen years in this house, but close to two decades total. I was employed by his uncle when he arrived as an orphan at the age of twelve. I wasn't even twenty, but I took him under my wing as best I could. Feeding a man for so long creates a bond."

I knew it was more than the food that tied them together. There was an emotional connection—trust and love. I didn't need to speak the words. Althea saw in my eyes that I understood.

"Her cook," Althea continued, "lost her apartment and had to move in with relatives. She's found work now, but it took a while with her not wanting to use Mrs. Snodgrass as a reference. She swore the woman killed her husband."

"It's an unsettled household," I remarked.

"Does the mister roam the halls?"

"Not that I've seen, but the only time I feel comfortable is when I'm in the kitchen or with Alvin in our rooms."

"Mr. Snodgrass probably didn't want to stick around that woman," Althea said with bluntness.

"It wouldn't be as nice as being around someone like Sean, would it?"

She shook her head. "I wish Sean Francis had a nice girl like you. Maybe he'll be able to find one after you banish Eliza."

We talked for so long, I didn't have time to visit Sean's library, but I promised to return with Alvin for supper on Friday.

At home, I slipped in the back door to avoid Catherine. After checking the apple pie was still in one piece, I reset my hair and settled in a rocking chair on the front porch.

It was almost half an hour before Alvin came down the street. His broad shoulders were squared as typical, but there was a dejected feeling to his gait. Hurrying down the front walk, I met him at the picket fence between the yards. I linked my arm under his that didn't carry his supplies.

Once we were in the front door, I took his lunchbox and satchel and helped him out of his suit jacket. Only then did I embrace him and meet his lips.

"Welcome home, Alvin." I smiled up at him, relishing his perfect grin when it came.

"Thank you, Deb."

"Come relax for a few minutes."

Alvin brought his bag and jacket to our sitting room, and I motioned him to my chair by the window. I removed his tie, then his shoes. He took hold of my hips and gently pulled me closer until I sat sideways on his lap. There he laid kisses across my forehead and down to my right ear.

"I never thought holding a wife would bring peace to my day, but it has."

"I'm happy to be of service, Alvin. It's a small token of return for all you give me." I curled against his shoulder knowing he would talk when he was ready.

"Principal Gentry wants me to redo my lesson plans. He says they're too advanced—that none of the teachers have been able to successfully teach polynomial equations before Christmas."

I stroked his arm. "He obviously never had a teacher of your caliber in his math department."

Alvin chuckled. "The other math instructors are old and set in their ways, though the female teacher for the girls' class is bright. Not that he pays a fraction of the attention to them that he gives to the boys' courses. Ms. Millwright, the math instructor, dropped off her lesson plan during my meeting with him. He flipped the pages, called his secretary in, and told her to pass the word to Ms. Millwright that it was fine. But mine he picked apart as too progressive and advanced."

"I bet he thought he was getting the old standards by recruiting a teacher from a private school."

"He didn't recruit me, Deb. I applied for the position."

I blinked as I watched him. There were no messages of remorse or fraud.

"You told me you accepted a job here. I assumed it was one they reached out to you with an offer for."

"They did, after I had applied."

"When?"

"June, at the close of the school year."

"Why didn't you tell me, Alvin?"

"We were barely acquaintances then. Why should I have announced to you I applied for a teaching position in Mobile?"

"When we started courting, you could have mentioned it on one of our walks. A 'by the way, Miss Alder, I really like you, but I might be moving soon.'"

"I knew it was a possibility. That's why I wanted to keep my distance, in case I did end up moving. You're so pretty, Deb. I didn't want to have my heart broken if I left."

"That's why you were reluctant to step out with me?"

"In part, but you snared me, in spite of my plans to protect myself."

I laughed and kissed him deeply as my hands roamed his shoulders. I was opening his shirt buttons when he stood with me in his arms.

"Are you bringing me to our bed?"

He nodded and claimed another kiss, causing me to giggle. Then there were footsteps in the hall outside our door.

"Did Alvin make it home?" Catherine called.

His hold on me loosened as he cleared his throat. "Yes, Cathy. I'm here."

"I'd love to chat. Don't keep me waiting too long."

"We'll be down soon."

"Not too soon," I whispered though I knew the mood was broken.

Catherine's shoes clipped down the stairs and Alvin set me on the bed.

"She did that on purpose."

"Don't get fanciful, Deb. I've enjoyed this time with you, but it *is* getting late." Alvin removed his shirt and went for the bathroom to wash.

I was disappointed that there was no promise to resume our activities later, but then I remembered Alvin wasn't one to talk about intimate things before they happened. He had wanted me in the bed, and I was certain we would have a union of body and soul sooner rather than later.

Downstairs, we sat together on the loveseat across from Catherine. She was over-dressed in her attempt to outshine me. Her décolletage would always be more remarkable, and she probably wore the evening gown for that specific purpose.

"You must feel accomplished after another day on the job, Alvin." Catherine smiled.

"It's good to be back to work."

"Tell us, Deborah, where did you spend your afternoon? You ran off after dinner and were gone several hours."

"I really don't think you'd be interested, Aunt Catherine."

"Certainly Alvin would be, or did you discuss that upstairs?"

"No, we didn't," Alvin replied. "Did you meet a new friend, Deb?"

"Yes. I went over to introduce myself to Althea. We'll be having supper there on Friday at eight, but she said to arrive any time after seven."

Alvin patted my hand. "I look forward to it."

"Who is this woman?" Catherine questioned. "Why have I never heard of her?"

"Althea is Sean Spunner's housekeeper," I said. "We've been invited to utilize his library, and I was to check with Althea about the best day for Alvin and I to come over for supper. We'll be out Friday evening, Aunt Catherine. I hope you'll get along without us."

Her chin went up. "This is the man who gave you a ride yesterday?"

"Yes, Mr. Spunner and Althea are the only people I've met so far."

"You cannot keep befriending single men and the help, Deborah. Did your parents not raise you better? I thought principals were stern."

"She's not into any mischief, Cathy," Alvin said in my defense.

"Time will be the judge of that," she sniped.

Seven

Thursday afternoon, I took the streetcar to the shopping district. In my reticule, I had the bridal money my parents had given me—the balance of what they had expected to spend on a lavish wedding for their only daughter rather than the small, speedily-planned backyard affair they'd held for me and Alvin the week previous. My goal was to buy a gorgeous evening gown.

I hesitated before the window display at Mademoiselle Bisset's shop, imagining myself wearing one of the colorful silk gowns with a shockingly low neckline. When Althea told me supper would be formal, I had asked her opinion on where to go. She sent me to this very French dress shop. Knowing Althea wouldn't lead me astray, I opened the door and breezed inside with a smile.

"Now this is what I like to see—a young lady who is unashamedly happy." A woman in a classic tailored black dress clapped her hands. "Welcome, my dear, I am Mademoiselle Bisset, and I will personally outfit you for any occasion."

"Thank you for the warm welcome. Your shop was recommended to me for a supper engagement I'll be attending with my husband tomorrow."

She nodded as she circled me in the open area between the counter and the seating area. "That is a short timeline, but you appear to be of a size that will not need many alterations."

"Oh, I hadn't thought of that. I'm not used to formal city occasions. We're new in town and have met one of your friendly solicitors."

"And who is the gentleman of the law that is so welcoming to new faces?"

"Mr. Sean Spunner."

"That dear man! I was to outfit his bride for their wedding, but she was lost the season before. Not a soul has turned his head in all these years, which is most unfortunate. What does your husband do, Mrs.…."

"Farley. Mrs. Alvin Farley. He's the newest math teacher at Barton Academy." I held my chin up, for no matter how humble his profession, Alvin was a man to be proud of. "I'd like a gown to last me through the next few seasons. Something I can easily alter with accessories to be worn for several occasions, should they arise."

"I am happy to do this for you, Mrs. Farley. Does your husband have a favorite color?"

"He loves all blues."

"That works favorably for your complexion." She pursed her lips a moment in contemplation. "I have a Jeanne Hallée I think will do well for you."

Within a curtained dressing room, Mademoiselle Bisset took my measurements and sent a shop girl to fetch the appropriate foundation garments. Once those were on, she helped me into the silk gown. It followed the curve of my hips and billowed around my feet, creating the mimic of a train without the fuss. The scrolling, deep blue damask print reached my wrists on sheer sleeves, but the back was a V-cut and a false underlay of cream covered in glass beads held a scooped neckline that was low enough to be intriguing. It even blended with the purple glow that surrounded me like a halo whenever I looked in a mirror.

"It's marvelous, mademoiselle!"

"I must agree with you. You carry it perfectly, my dear. Now allow me to find a pair of shoes…"

When I left the store, it was with a receipt for the gown, foundation pieces, multiple pairs of silk hosiery, plus one pair of shoes, and a nightgown—all to be delivered the following morning.

Still having close to forty dollars in my purse, I stopped next at First National Bank where Alvin had an account.

I waited in line until I was called to the counter.

"I'm Mrs. Alvin Farley," I told the clerk. "My husband banks here. I'm not sure of the account number, but I can give you our address. I wanted to deposit thirty dollars as a surprise to him."

"Of course, Mrs. Farley. Just a moment."

The clerk returned from pulling his file with an eager smile. He practically fell over himself while recording my deposit. It was a healthy amount, but not worth the fuss he was giving it.

"Let your husband know that he only needs to stop in and sign a note granting you permission to withdraw from the account up to a set amount to give you spending money when you need it." He slid the deposit slip across the counter to me.

I folded the paper and slipped it into my bag. "Thank you."

Utilizing the streetcars, I managed to arrive home before Alvin. We had an almost-pleasant evening downstairs with Catherine, though I had to once again explain my absence from the house. I did so without revealing my special purposes or the forgotten deposit slip in my bag.

Friday morning, I made a batch of butter cookies— something that would keep well since we were dining at Sean's house. When my delivery from Mademoiselle Bisset arrived, Catherine looked like she wanted to tear the striped boxes out of my hands.

"Does Alvin know you're wasting money on over-priced French ensembles?"

"It's a surprise for our supper out."

"So you bought new clothes for Mr. Spunner's benefit?"

"I did no such thing, Aunt Catherine." I went for the stairs. "Besides, you're always harping about me needing to look presentable. I'd have thought you'd be pleased."

"Not when you're being frivolous with Alvin's money!"

I stopped before the window on the landing and turned. "I bought all this with *my* money."

Her hands went to her full hips. "I had no idea *you* were an heiress."

"I'm not. It was a wedding gift, if you must know. It took my father years to save up what he did. My family never lacked anything, but we didn't employ multiple servants." I met her cold gaze. "I know I'm not what you want in your life, but I assure you Alvin is happy with me."

She frowned and disappeared into the parlor.

I retreated upstairs and focused on the joy of unwrapping my purchases. It was like my birthday but tenfold as I'd never experienced such opulence. The new underclothes and shapewear, the shoes and dress. Tucked into a little box within the package with my silk nightgown was a note and pair of drop crystal earrings.

Mrs. Farley,

Please accept these earrings as a "Welcome to Mobile" gift. They are a fine piece of costume jewelry, tasteful enough to wear before the most discerning eyes. And they will look ravishing with your new dress, though your classic pearls do the job too.

I am glad you found your way to my shop.

I happily removed the pearl studs I always wore and hooked in the sparkling earrings. It instantly brought allure to my face and would look well against a bare neck.

I forced myself to wait until after three before beginning to wash and dress. I wanted to surprise Alvin when he returned, but not in front of Catherine. Glittering from head to toe, I watched for his return from the sitting room window.

When Alvin passed under me to the front porch, I heard the titter of Catherine welcoming him home. The minutes ticked by as the murmur of voices and laughter continued from downstairs. Perhaps it was my growing annoyance or my feeling of aloneness as Alvin continued on with Catherine that pricked my sensitivity, but for the first time I felt a message within my sanctuary.

Do not trust her.

I almost answered aloud that I didn't, for I knew it was in regards to the woman downstairs. The urge to run to Alvin overwhelmed me. Instead, I paced the room to expel the frustration seething through me over my husband's delay.

It was nearly six before Alvin came up the stairs. Exhaling my disappointment over the long wait, I paused beside his desk so the lamp would shine on the beadwork across my bodice.

He stopped just inside the room, mouth slack from surprise. I waited for him to speak—preferably apologizing for his tardiness—but he only blinked.

"Good evening, Alvin," I finally said. "I've been waiting for your return. I hope you had a great finish to your work week."

Still nothing.

He watched as if under a spell as I crossed the room—eyes roving my form.

I touched his arm, noting his jacket was missing, and he was scented with Catherine's perfume. "Why didn't you come to me sooner?"

"Cathy told me you were on a walk, so I waited downstairs for your return." His gaze dropped to the expanse of my skin on display. Raising a hand, his finger traveled the scoop of the trim on the cream fabric from one shoulder to the other. Then his hands lifted to my face and he left the whisper of a kiss on my lips. "My wife, the most beautiful woman in the world."

Not able to refute his sincerity, though I thought him beyond exaggeration, I smiled. He appeared too awed to smile back, choosing to continue his study of my new items from my earrings to my shoes.

"You're perfect, Deb. And to think I missed another hour with you."

I didn't want to speak badly of his aunt, so I spoke of the future. "We have from this moment on."

Our lips met with fervor. Alvin's hands traveled the damask patterns down my arms then followed it around my hips as we continued our heated embrace.

When he pulled back for breath, his gaze softened. "If I go into the next room to prepare for supper, will you still be here when I return?"

"Yes, Alvin."

"I'm afraid you'll disappear—that I might wake up and find myself alone."

I gathered his large hands and pressed his knuckles to my lips as I looked up at him. "Ever since my father's party last year, I've wanted to be yours. I enjoy my role as Mrs. Alvin Robert Farley too much to ever leave you."

His grin shone, filling me with light.

While he prepared for our evening out, I sat in the chair by the window, working on my knitted shawl. It kept me from marching to Catherine and letting her know what I thought of her waylaying Alvin.

We descended the stairs at seven. Alvin, wearing his charcoal gray three-piece wedding suit, proudly escorted me into the parlor.

"Isn't she beautiful, Cathy?" he asked. "Deborah surprised me with the new gown. I think I'll be forced to buy a tuxedo so I can match her style next time."

"But you look handsome, Alvin," she said from the settee as she checked me from high pompadour to proper slippers. "You don't need to feel inferior next to someone playing dress up."

"I—I'm not sure how late we'll be," he stammered, "so don't feel you need to wait up for us."

On the sidewalk, Alvin's arm went around my waist. "I'm sorry about Cathy's sharpness. I don't think she understands how she comes across."

"Doesn't she?" I asked pointedly. "She's been antagonistic to me since I arrived. I know when I'm not wanted, Alvin. Please do me a favor. If I'm not waiting on the porch for you in the afternoons, seek me out right away."

"Of course."

"And know I'll never leave word with Catherine about anything. I've been told on good authority she's not to be trusted."

At Sean's house, our host welcomed us at the door as a ragtime tune played cheerily from inside. Sean wore a black tuxedo and a friendly smile. Eyes brightening at the sight of me, he pulled me into the house at the same time the shadow behind him zipped up the stairs.

"If I'm not mistaken, Deborah, this has the touch of Mademoiselle Bisset."

"You're exactly right." I smiled in return. "Thank you for having us, Sean. I hope we aren't too much trouble."

"Nonsense." He quickly kissed my cheek and turned to shake Alvin's hand. "I don't entertain nearly as much as I'd like. Do you dance, Deborah?"

"Of course. I did attend finishing school, even if I was raised in the country."

Sean looked to Alvin again. "May I borrow your wife?"

He nodded, lips in a thin line.

"Would you like a shot of something now or wait until later?"

"Later, thank you," Alvin replied.

"Make yourself comfortable, Alvin." Sean motioned into the front room before taking my arm.

The phonograph was in the wide hall near the stairs, strategically placed so the paneled area would carry the tune to most of the house from the central location. I followed his lead in a cake walk until the tune ended. Then Sean changed the recordings and a traditional waltz started.

"I'd like one with you as well, Alvin," I called to him as Sean spun me around the polished wood floor with natural grace.

Alvin nodded, eyes never leaving me.

"Did you invite someone else to join us?" I asked Sean.

"Tonight is about getting to know the two of you better. Besides, I didn't know if you would want to be surrounded by more men, as another invitation would probably be a bachelor friend."

"I have two brothers, and my father runs a boys' school. I couldn't get away from men if I tried."

"That's good to know." He danced me to Alvin in the parlor. "Take the next song, then I'll show y'all the house."

I leaned close, swaying with Alvin to the dreamy music as he led us in a box step.

"Happy one week anniversary, Deb."

"I didn't think of that," Sean said when the music stopped. "How was your first week together?"

"Glorious," Alvin said without pause.

Sean grinned. "I bet."

I put my arms around Alvin. "A wonderful adventure."

"It's been a lot of changes for you." Sean put a hand on each of our shoulders. "I'm pleased to have met you so soon after your arrival. Now come see the house. It will be fresh for both of you because Althea swears Deborah only went to the kitchen the other day."

"We chatted like old friends and ate the cookies she'd made for you."

"Althea managed to save me a few." Sean winked. "Let's begin upstairs."

There were two guest bedrooms plus an enormous master suite which Sean proudly entered.

It was odd going into a man's bedroom, even with Alvin holding my hand, but I knew in an instant why Sean wanted us to see it. Over the carved mantel was a portrait that could be none other than his lost love. The figure in the gilt frame looked over her naked shoulder at the viewer, holding a purple drape to her chest as she smiled seductively. Her long, dark hair tumbled down her bare back, her penetrating eyes daring anyone to speak ill of her boldness.

"Eliza Rose Melling," Sean said with reverence. "She was nineteen when she painted this self-portrait for me. Her talent and beauty defied everything."

"To see her fully in color…" My voice trailed off before I realized I'd said the words aloud.

Alvin was too busy staring to hear, but Sean grinned, utilizing his full arsenal of dimples. He looked like a love-sick schoolboy. It was no wonder he couldn't forget her. It might even be him that was unwittingly keeping her bound.

A cold wind swept the room but it did little to cool Alvin's blush as he studied the painting. The current pulled me to the wall to the right of the bathroom door where a collection of smaller framed sketches hung. They were eye-level with the nearby bed. Approaching them, I realized the intricate sketches were nudes of his departed fiancée from various angles.

Alvin came to my side. "Deborah, why are you looking at those?"

Sean laughed and clapped Alvin's shoulder. "It's nothing either of you haven't seen before on another woman. But enough of the peep show. You still need to see the library."

I was safely on Alvin's arm as we returned to the main floor, but unease followed me or—more likely—Eliza did.

The rich wood space of the library was scented with pipe tobacco. Bookcases filled three of the walls. A tufted leather chaise was in one corner, a desk in another.

"What an excellent room!" Alvin released my arm and went for the small gaming table with a chess board in front of the window. "And a gorgeous set."

"The pieces are marble. My uncle gave it to me last Christmas, but I haven't played in months." Sean brushed my hand when he stopped beside me. "Would you mind, Deborah, if Alvin and I play after supper?"

"Not at all."

"You would have free roaming privileges while we play. I'm sure you could find a book or two that would interest you."

He pointed out his small section of mathematic books to Alvin, most of them old school texts. I sat on one of the armchairs at the inlaid chess board and watched them chatting like old friends. Sean practically lived like a king in this house of art, music, and books. He should have shared it with a wife and children by now—his own kingdom in the Port City—save for the spirit of Eliza. Then I imagined the fullness of life and freedom Alvin and I would be allowed if we had a home of our own, but that was more unlikely than banishing Eliza.

The resonate sound of a gong rippled through the house.

"That's the call to the supper table," Sean said. "Allow me to escort you, Deborah."

The table was set on one end with both side settings close to the head seat. A vase with orange and white roses was in the true center of the table so as not to block our view of each other. Pleased with the intimate setting, I smiled at Alvin across from me and then our host.

Sean prayed in gratitude for the food and company, then Althea came through the door.

"Good evening, Mr. and Mrs. Farley," she said as she balanced a tray.

"Hello, Althea. Please call me Deborah as you did before. And my husband is Alvin."

She nodded her head to us as she dispersed salad plates to us all with a dainty scoop of crab salad. "As you like, Miss Deborah. Mr. Alvin, I hope you know what a gem you have with this woman."

"I do, thank you."

Later, after Althea delivered the blackened shrimp and sautéed asparagus, I looked to Sean. "Am I showing poor manners by chatting with your cook?"

Sean laughed. "I'd be offended if you didn't. In my house, Althea isn't hired help, she's family."

"Good." I smiled with relief. "I'd love to come back and visit her."

"You and Alvin are welcome anytime."

After eating raspberry cream cake, we returned to the library. While Alvin settled at the chess board, Sean took my elbow and brought me to a far bookcase. He removed a volume and set it reverently in my hands.

The Book on Mediums: Guide for Mediums and Invocators by Allan Kardec.

"This is an English translation from its original French. I looked it over again this week and I'm certain that mediumship is your gift. Take it with you if you wish," he whispered.

I nodded, but knew I couldn't carry it home without Alvin seeing it, and I wasn't ready for him to know. Settled on the chaise to read the introduction, I tried concentrating, but it felt like Eliza was throwing darts at me.

A prick to my spine.

A flick on my arm.

"Please stop," I muttered. "You should be more mature than this."

When a touch as cold as a northerly wind in January went down my back, I snapped the book shut. Alvin briefly looked at me and smiled before returning his concentration to the board, but Sean watched me cross the room.

I followed Eliza's promptings to the bookcase behind Sean's desk.

Third shelf, right side.

A tall, thin book.

As I pulled it free, Sean laughed.

"I know my move wasn't as terrible as that," Alvin said with indignation.

"It's not you." Sean went for the arsenal of beverages on a brass cart near the chaise and poured himself a whisky. "Would you like a dash, Alvin?"

"The game will only be fair if I do."

Sean delivered a glass to Alvin and came to me with a swaggering gait. "Out of all the books in this room, Deborah!"

"Yes?" I raised my eyebrows and set my fingers on the edge of the cover to open it.

"I wouldn't do that if I were you."

"Eliza wanted me to—"

"I'm sure she did, the little seductress." He took a sip of whisky and set the glass on the desk. Leaning closer, his breath tickled my ear. "She's trying to shock you. It's a book on sexual positions."

I thrust the book at him. He tucked it back onto the shelf, collected his glass, and returned to his game.

When we walked home an hour later. Alvin's arm was around my waist, his hand on my hip uncharacteristically firm.

Alvin stopped on the path to the front porch of the house. Under an inky sky speckled with stars, he held me to his chest. "I can tell you and Sean have some common bond, but I don't want you getting emotionally involved with him, Deborah."

"Even if I want to help lift someone out of suffering, I need no other than you for my life's fulfillment, Alvin." I hugged him tight, hoping he didn't realize I was withholding something from him that I had shared with Sean.

Eight

Saturday, Alvin and I were together in our sitting room most of the morning, then Catherine roped him into helping in the yard after the noon dinner.

Perhaps I should have chaperoned, but I couldn't tolerate her false enthusiasm for a birdbath and benches while she eyed Alvin's backside as he moved the things around the rose garden. Instead, I expelled my annoyance by whipping up a batch of banana pudding while Tessa scrubbed the pantry floor. Catherine's tinkling laughter came through the open windows, but I did my best to ignore it.

"How do you like working here?" I asked Tessa after she came back from dumping the dirty water in the side yard.

Her narrow face pulled into a grimace, but when she saw my earnestness she relaxed. "Not very well, but it's better now that you and Mr. Farley are here."

"Mrs. Snodgrass likes to make a spectacle, doesn't she?"

She nodded and glanced nervously to the backdoor. "I don't see how you stand listening to her. She's shameless."

"Shameless in many things, I imagine."

Tessa's face reddened.

"Did you know her before working here?"

She shook her head. "She saw me—came across me downtown one day."

The image of Tessa pocketing a pair of silk hosiery inside a department store filled my head.

"She forced you into service, didn't she?" I whispered.

Tessa lowered her blue eyes and nodded. "I made one mistake in my life—all to look pretty for a man—but she caught me. It was either work for her or she'd turn me into the store, who would telephone the police. I had to quit my bakery job to work here for less pay but more hours."

I didn't go so far as to verbally doubt a department store would involve the police over a pair of stockings since she didn't share that information with me, but I nodded my understanding.

"I'm not wicked, Mrs. Farley."

"I know you aren't. We all make mistakes."

She smiled, and I removed the apron I'd worn to protect my mauve skirt and white blouse. Before I could go for the yard, there was a knock on the front door.

Sean Spunner stood on the porch, a black derby in hand and a sheepish grin on his face.

"Good afternoon, Deborah."

"Hello, Sean." I motioned him inside, happy to see Eliza's shadow stayed on the front walk. "You're just in time to help me rescue Alvin from his aunt's clutches."

Sean laughed. "I'll do my best. Why didn't you take the Kardec book with you?"

I placed his hat on the mirrored rack in the hall. "I don't want Alvin to see it. I'll come over while he's at work to read. Althea won't mind, will she?"

"Of course not. Now where's Alvin?"

Sean followed me down the hall to the back of the house. We silently stepped onto the screened porch. Alvin sat on the newly moved bench—barely visible though the blooming roses—and Catherine leaned provocatively over him, breasts bound within her red dress on level with his face.

Sean gave a low *tsk*. "Clutches are right. Allow me to attempt to draw her attention, for Alvin's sake."

He held the screen door, and I enthusiastically descended the back steps.

"Alvin, we have a visitor!"

Catherine straightened as Alvin stood, adjusting his collar. He was without a tie, having removed it before going outside, but still buttoned to the top even though his sleeves were rolled to his elbows.

"Hello, Sean," Alvin called as we crunched over the oyster-shell path toward him. After shaking hands, he turned to his aunt. "May I introduce my aunt, Catherine Snodgrass. Cathy, this is Sean Spunner, whom Deborah and I dined with last night."

"Mr. Spunner." She inclined her head to him after a flash of annoyance at me.

"It is a pleasure, Mrs. Snodgrass." Sean took her hand and kissed the back of it. "Please excuse my oversight in not extending an invitation to you. I was under the impression that you were in mourning, but I don't see a speck of black on you."

"Black doesn't suite me, Mr. Spunner."

"It never does on a vivacious woman." He winked. "Would you be so kind as to show me your roses? They're stunning even this late in the season."

After a quick appraisal of his stature, Catherine offered her arm.

Sean tucked it around his with a caressing motion and pointed to the furthest bush. "Shall we begin with these?"

I took Alvin's hand and led him to the back stoop. The jaunty suspenders accented his broad shoulders and narrow hips more than typical, and I couldn't resist touching him. Standing a step up so we were the same height, I unhooked his top button and kissed his neck.

"Deb, there's a guest here." He gently brushed my hand away, but was grinning.

"Yes, and he's kind enough to entertain your aunt so you could return to me." Arms around his shoulders, I leaned in as my lips sought a connection with his.

Alvin yielded to my embrace, adding his own to our entanglement. Hands on my back, I felt their heat through my shirtwaist as he pulled me tighter to him. I deepened the kiss and he nearly groaned into my mouth. After a nibbling tug on my lower lip, he nuzzled my ear.

"You're a bad influence on me." His hands roamed to my waist, then up my sides in a sensuous tease that cause me to arch against him.

"We're married, Alvin. There's nothing wrong with craving each other."

"Not in the middle of the afternoon with an audience across the yard." Noticing my frown, he kissed me before lifting me into a hug. "But I love you, Deb. You know that."

"I like to be reminded."

Alvin's smile lines showed when he grinned at me. He took my hand as we walked back to the rose garden, and the fullness of my love for him erupted with a weightless gaiety that I wanted to hold forever. Catherine immediately looked at us, though she kept talking to Sean, who played the role of an ardent suitor well with his flirty banter and welcoming body language.

You are to blame.

I felt Eliza behind me and concentrated my thoughts in an attempt to communicate with her in return.

The woman is nothing to him. Don't be jealous, Eliza.

He's doing it for you.

He rescued Alvin.

This display is for you. It will come back to haunt you.

I shivered as an icy breath traveled my spine .

Alvin dropped my hand and hugged me. "Do you have a chill?"

His brown eyes were filled with concern.

"Not with you as my wrap."

While we were kissing, Sean brought Catherine over. Alvin released our connection and stood beside me, holding my hand.

"Aren't they the best matched couple, Mrs. Snodgrass?" Sean asked. "I've never seen a handsomer pair. I can easily imagine them on the dance floor at a Mardi Gras masquerade. Do you attend?"

"My late husband wasn't a member of any societies, but we were invited to several balls during our time together."

Sean turned to us. "Say the word, Alvin, and I'll see you receive invitations this winter."

"Thank you." Alvin released his grip on me. "We're happy to see you, Sean, but was there something special you needed?"

"I just wanted to tell you and Deborah how much I enjoyed last night. Stop by whenever you wish a chess match or to borrow a book."

"Shall we see you to the door?" I asked.

"Thank you, but I'm fine with the side gate, Deborah."

"But your hat. I'll get it for you."

When I returned a moment later, the men were in discussion, Catherine's shrewd eyes moving between the two as if comparing meat in a butcher's window. Maybe Sean's carefree charm would be more to her liking, but Alvin's earnest presence was forever etched in my heart.

***

At supper on Sunday, there was a red glow around Catherine to accompany her pointed tongue.

"I saw Mr. Spunner drive by this afternoon in his automobile while I was on the front porch. He waved to me and flashed that disarming smile. He's not the type of person I figured you would befriend, Alvin."

Alvin looked up from the roast he was carving. "Why is that, Cathy? He's educated and cultured. Not to mention kind."

"Those things he might be, but he seems rather a fast one. I wouldn't think you'd want your wife around a man like that."

Alvin speared into the green beans on his plate. "He's friendly and closer in age to me than any of the male teachers on staff at Barton."

"But what of the female teachers in the girls' school?" Catherine asked.

"There are some in their twenties—about half, I'd say. They're nice enough, but I don't think it's appropriate for me to encourage friendship with them."

Catherine flashed me a malicious smile. "Deborah is the jealous type, is she? Then why doesn't she think you might feel the same way about her befriending men?"

"Sean Spunner is a gentleman, the same as Alvin," I said with conviction. "He's never given me cause for concern."

"So you relish flirtations?" she quipped.

"If you're referring to how he was with you yesterday afternoon, Aunt Catherine, I can assure you he's never behaved that way toward me. You're closer to his age and a single woman, while I'm married and more than a decade his junior."

She took a sip of wine and mulled over that thought. "How old is he?"

"Thirty this past spring," Alvin answered.

"And his financial standing?"

"Solid, from what I can tell. Finnigan and Spunner, his uncle's law firm which he's a senior partner in, is one of the most respected in the city, and his home is richly furnished." Alvin took another bite after speaking, studying her as he did so. "Don't tell me you're ready to move on from Uncle Jerald."

"Alvin, dear, Jerald was a wonderful man, but a woman cannot be expected to be alone forever. Having you here has reminded me what comforts a man brings to a home."

He blushed, and set to eating without further word until Tessa brought in the tray with my apple tarts and fresh whipped cream. When she set his plate before him, Alvin smiled.

"You've outdone yourself, Deborah. This looks delicious."

I squeezed his knee beneath the table. "I hope you enjoy it."

As typical, Catherine tried to look displeased during dessert, though she ate everything on her plate. Maybe she was privy to the old saying about the way to a man's heart was through his stomach.

When we were changing for bed, Alvin caught me around the waist. He nosed into my loose hair and kissed below my ear.

"I love you, Alvin," I whispered.

His kisses traveled lower, and he led us toward the bed without breaking his attentions. Every day, he grew bolder with his passions, but he was still a silent lover. The sweetest, most tender-hearted husband I could ever imagine. I matched his quiet loving with an equally hushed reverence whenever we joined, but I still wished for moments of wild passion.

The next morning, I saw Alvin off to work, then cleaned what we used for breakfast and retreated upstairs to avoid Catherine. I made our bed with fresh sheets, dusted, and swept our space.

Wanting to be ready to leave the house after our midday meal, I pulled out the purse I'd last used when I went to town Thursday. Sitting on the end of the bed, I dumped the contents out so I could straighten them. My clasped money pouch still held five dollars plus change. A small notebook and pen, should I need to write something down. A miniature brush and mirror. And the deposit receipt from the bank I'd forgotten to tell Alvin about.

I carried it to his desk and smoothed the folded paper. Proud of my thirty dollar contribution to our future, I glanced at the handwritten total expecting to see a hundred or two because Alvin wasn't frivolous with money.

$40,253.74

I looked at it again, running a finger over the ink. Where did Alvin get money in that amount? Was it a mistake on the bank's part? If it wasn't, and Alvin had that amount at his disposal, why on earth were we living with Aunt Catherine?

Confused and angry, I threw myself into the chair and starred out the window as if the answer would come to me from the puffy clouds in the blue sky.

Sometime later, a knock sounded on the sitting room door.

"Miss Deborah?" Tessa called. "Are you coming down for dinner?"

The clock on the mantel said it was five after twelve.

"Yes, thank you." I smoothed my dress and opened the door. "I'll be there as soon as I wash."

When I sat at the table, Catherine took a sip from her iced tea.

"I hope you didn't expect me to wait for you."

"No, Aunt Catherine. I'm sorry I'm late. I got distracted." I took a spoonful of soup.

"It's amazing you find things to occupy yourself with in that room most of the day. Are you playing dolls or other childish games?"

"I don't need to answer that."

Catherine laughed, her brown eyes mysterious as though she held knowledge. Did she know about Alvin's stash of money? Is that why she was overly friendly with him?

For the first time I yearned to hear a message from the other side, but all was silent. Could I force the spirits to speak? Perhaps the book at Sean's house held the answers to that. I planned to escape there as soon as I finished eating.

Upstairs, I tucked the bank receipt back into my reticule before hurrying out.

Althea answered my knock at Sean's house. "Good afternoon, Miss Deborah. Sean Francis is at work," she said with a smile, "but you didn't come for him."

"I'm here to read a book he showed me Friday night." I followed her into the house.

"He told me you have permission to borrow anything from the library."

"I know, but I don't want Alvin to see it. Would it be inconvenient if I read it here in the afternoons?"

"It won't bother me one bit, child. I like your company. Shall I bring in something for you to drink?"

"I just finished dinner, but thank you."

"A treat in another hour or two then. Make yourself comfortable."

"In the event I get too absorbed in reading, would you nudge me at three-thirty so I can make it home by four?"

"That's no problem. You take your time in there."

The Alan Kardec book waited for me on the table beside the chaise. Sticking out of the front cover was a note.

Deborah,

I am leaving this in hopes you will return. Yes, it is selfish on my part because I wish you to help Eliza, but also because I enjoy my time with you and Alvin. Though I suppose I will not see you if you come to read while he is at work. All the same, know that my kindest thoughts go out to you. Ask Althea for whatever you wish. She has instructions to see to your every comfort when you visit.

Sincerely,

Sean

Feeling at peace with the welcome extended to me, I set the note aside and removed my walking boots. I curled up on the leather chaise with the book and started on the first chapter.

Thoughts of Alvin's secret money tried to overtake my concentration, but I struggled through the first sections before Althea arrived with a coffee tray. Filled with jumbled emotions as I was, I didn't invite her to join me. I read for another hour before Alvin completely took over my thinking. The spirits had never lied to me and the message from his soul the day we meet was nothing short of perfection for an honest young man. The missive about Alvin Robert Farley was one of safety and trust. What could have gone wrong in the year since then?

I was crying when Sean came in the door.

"Dear God, what is it, Deborah?" He dropped to a knee before me, taking me by the shoulders.

The concern on his face split me more. I didn't try to stop the tears or his embrace when he settled on the chaise.

"Althea!"

When she appeared, he instructed her to ready a touch of brandy. A little glass was soon in my hands.

I drank, swallowing the as best I could in my upset state.

"There, there." He stroked my back. "What in the book upset you?"

I shook my head and wiped my nose with the handkerchief he'd given me.

"Not the book? Did Eliza do something to you?"

A strangled laugh broke through. "She didn't come until you did, but with the feelings rippling from her"—I pointed to where her shadow hovered by his desk—"I wouldn't be surprised if she tried to drown me. She doesn't like you comforting me."

"Am I bringing comfort, Deborah?" His face held a look of expectation then relief when I nodded. "Good. You looked completely distraught. What is it?"

I straightened my dress and wiped my face. "I found out a secret Alvin's been hiding from me."

I took a deep breath and explained about wanting to surprise Alvin by adding my money to the bank, then forgetting the deposit slip until that morning. "Do you think they wrote down the wrong balance?"

"I doubt First National would make a mistake like that. Would you like me to check to be sure?"

"You can do that?"

"Darling, you have no idea the connections I have in this city. But to make it official, do you have the account number?"

I pulled the receipt from my bag and handed it to him.

He whistled at the total. The new-model candlestick-style telephone was brought to the front of his desk when he sat with ease, the earpiece lifted. Once the operator connected him to the bank, his posture straightened.

"Yes, I need the manager right away." A pause. "Solicitor Spunner. Thank you."

"Hello, Melvin. How are you doing today?" After a bit of small talk, and a lot of smiles, Sean settled back on the course. "Listen, I've got a potential client, and I was hoping you could do me the favor of quietly verifying an account balance for me."

He gave him Alvin's name and account number.

Then we waited what seemed like an hour for the banker to come back.

"Thank you, Melvin. You've been most helpful." A laugh. "Yes, he'll be able to handle any fees I throw at him. I'll see you at the club later this week. Good afternoon."

Sean hung the earpiece on the base and bit his lip.

"It's true, isn't it?" I said.

He nodded. "Your husband is richer than I am."

"But what does it mean? And why didn't he tell me? And more importantly, why are we living with his horrible aunt when he has the means of securing us our own home?"

"I don't know, Deborah, but I don't wish to think the worst of Alvin."

"Nor I! It defies everything I've felt about him. I don't know what to think or how to confront him, or even if I should. He knows how things are between Catherine and me. If he loved me, why would he make us stay when we could live elsewhere? Could he love her—love her more than me?"

"That's impossible, Deborah."

"Then what's behind this astronomical sum of money?"

Sean took my hands. "Is that a rhetorical question or do you wish me to help you discover the truth?"

He studied my face as the possibilities raced through my mind.

"I have to know, Sean. Will you please help me?"

Nodding, he gave me a sly smile. "You can count on me to get to the bottom of this."

Nine

When I walked home at four-thirty, Alvin was coming up the street. We met in front of the neighbor's house. His smile seemed as true as ever, but I couldn't help but feel it was a mask.

"Hello, Deb." He kissed my cheek. "Where have you been?"

"Reading at Sean's house. He has a European book, translated from French, that looks too expensive for me to want to risk bringing home in case something were to happen to it. Althea let me in, and I read in the library for a few hours."

"That's nice."

He didn't ask if I saw Sean, and I didn't offer more information. Were we both living a lie?

"How was school today?" I stopped on the front porch and motioned to the rocking chairs to see if he wanted to sit.

He pointed up, signaling he wanted to go to our rooms. Fortunately, Catherine wasn't in the parlor so we made it to the sitting room without trouble.

"The students have that beginning of the year boisterousness, coupled with testing out the new teacher." He removed his messenger bag and slumped into my chair by the front window.

"Were you stern with them?"

"Three of the classes, but they needed it." He grinned and held his hand out. He reeled me closer and tugged me onto his lap. "Just looking at you makes me feel relaxed."

"I hope I'm all you'll ever need, Alvin. You can talk to me about anything. Anything at all, and I'll do my best to be understanding."

"I know, Deb." He closed his eyes and embraced me. "You're a sensitive soul. It goes along with your vivid imagination."

I rested my head on his shoulder. When the supper bell rang, I reluctantly stood. Alvin's hand trailed down my back then gave my buttocks a playful squeeze.

"Alvin!" I laughed and turned to him.

"You're making me naughtier by the day, Deb." Alvin took my hand. "You aren't shocked, are you? You look upset."

"No, of course not." I leaned in for a quick kiss. "It pleasantly surprised me. I love being your wife, Alvin. You don't need to be shy around me."

"I'm learning that. Be patient with me."

My dress was a bit rumpled from being curled on Alvin's lap, and I'm sure we had an intimate glow about us when we entered the dining room. Catherine's eyes narrowed as she looked us over.

True to her vicious form, she started a battle as soon as the food was served. "Were you off to Mr. Spunner's house again today, Deborah?"

"I'm using his library while he's at work. His housekeeper lets me in."

"I saw him drive by on his way home over half an hour before I heard you and Alvin return. Did he meet you both there?"

"I met Alvin on the sidewalk in front of the house."

"So you were alone with Mr. Spunner. That's an interesting situation."

"We were never alone, and it was only a short overlap of time. Nothing clandestine or planned, Aunt Catherine. You make it sound shameful for no reason."

"The help is hardly a proper chaperone. Surely you see that, Alvin. If you don't teach her how to behave, the neighbors will talk about her."

Alvin's eyes cut from her to me, but he kept chewing.

"Aren't you worr—"

"Enough!" Alvin's harshness put a stop to Catherine's slander. "I don't like the way you speak of my wife, Cathy."

My hand went to his knee with a touch of thanks, but he didn't make eye contact. For the first time since our arrival, Catherine didn't ask us to stay in the parlor after dessert.

Alvin silently followed me upstairs.

"Deborah, I have to know," he said as soon as we were in our sitting room. "Is Sean behaving himself around you?"

"Yes, Alvin, completely. He's been a gentleman to me since we met in the park."

"And who spoke to whom first?"

I paused, thinking back on the afternoon over a week ago. "He did, but he saw me watching him. I heard his voice, warm and caring. I turned to the sound and watched him with the children he's friends with. I thought they were his family, and my thoughts were of you, how you would be just as kind and loving with our children as he was with them. And then I saw—it doesn't matter. I watched with curiosity. My heart only has room for you. I've never loved another—and never want to love another. Can't you see that Catherine is turning you against me?" I took his arm. "I've loved no man in my life but you. I may have had infatuations in my youth, but I've kissed only you. And since the day we met, you've been the only one I desire."

His eyes were cold as he stared at me. I silently pled for him to say something similar to me in return.

He shook his head. "Don't ask that of me, Deborah. I hear the truth in your words, but I can't say the same."

Alvin offered no explanation when he left. I dropped to the bed, turned my face into the pillow, and cried.

I woke when the door clicked shut. The room was dark, the residue of my stale tears stiff on my cheeks. I held my position, facing the curtained window. My shoes were kicked off but I was otherwise fully dressed, still atop the bedspread.

Alvin's shoes dropped to the floor, then the sound of his jacket and suspenders coming off followed. My body tensed, unsure what to expect as I listened to him disrobe.

Soon his knee was on the edge of the bed, dipping me towards him, so I rolled onto my back. His fingers worked the buttons on my shirt, breath hot on my face and perfumed with alcohol.

I opened my eyes, watching his shadowy form undress me. When the buttons were all seen to, he pulled me upright, leaning me against his bare chest as he peeled the clothing down my arms. As soon as it was off, I hugged him.

"Deb." He kissed from the hollow of my throat up to my lips. "I'm sorry. I didn't mean to hurt you. I shouldn't have left without explaining, leaving you to imagine the worst. It's not what you think, Deborah. There's no one else in my life now."

"You've been drinking. Where did you go?"

"Sean's house. He listened to my sorrows, poured whiskey while we talked, and told me to get back here and make love to you." He laughed. "He railed at me for walking out like I did."

I smiled against his chest. "Good."

"Do you forgive me, Deb?"

Nodding, I hugged Alvin tighter, determined to hold to him always.

***

The next afternoon, I returned to Sean's house to read more of the Kardec book. Alvin never confessed what love he was burdened with, but knowing it wasn't current was enough—for now. I was able to concentrate on the book, becoming deeply involved in the descriptions of the different types of mediums that the ringing of the telephone startled me.

Althea came to the door of the library. "Sean Francis is on the telephone for you. Take the line on his desk, and I'll hang up in the kitchen."

I settled at the desk and retrieved the earpiece, leaning toward the receiver. "Hello?"

"I won't be so crass as to ask how your night was, but I hope all is well."

The kitchen line clicked.

"Better than it was, Sean. Did Alvin tell you everything?"

"I believe he did. Are you reading, darling?"

"I was, thank you. What did Alvin tell you about his previous entanglements?"

"Now, now, Deborah. What men share while drinking deserves to be kept in confidence."

"But I must know! He told me it wasn't current, but—"

"Let that be enough."

"Sean, I thought you were on my side."

"Don't be a goose, Deborah. I'm on the Farleys' side—both you *and* Alvin. It's not a competition." He sighed. "Listen, if it will help you, I'll tell you one thing—1906 was a year of heartbreak for both me and Alvin."

"It's over a girl from four years ago?"

"Yes, Deborah. You have nothing to be jealous over, all right?"

"Fine, but what about the bank? Did you question him about that?"

"Heavens no! But I did do some digging today. I found out where the money is from. Once again, there's nothing you need to be concerned about."

"Allow me to be the judge of that."

Sean laughed. "You're a feisty one."

"If it's nothing illegal, why hasn't Alvin told me?"

"I have a theory, but it's only that. I suggest you stay patient until your strong, silent type is ready to talk."

"Sean, I could throttle you right now!"

"Then I'm glad I'm not there. Enjoy your reading time, darling."

The line clicked and I screamed my frustration.

Althea came to the door. "Ready for a coffee break?"

"I doubt I'll be able to concentrate anymore today." I followed Althea to the kitchen.

She was smiling when she set the table. "You and your husband are good for Sean Francis. I'm glad y'all found each other."

"He's been wonderful until today, but I suppose I can't complain because he's doing so much, even if he isn't telling me everything."

"If I had to guess, I'd say Sean Francis thinks these things would be best told to you from your husband." She sipped her coffee. "Have you discovered anything useful in the book?"

I nodded. "Yes, clarity. For much of my life, I never knew what I was experiencing and the past few years was guesswork for something I thought I was alone in. I don't feel so odd anymore."

She nodded. "I'm sure that's a comfort."

"It is. And I'm going to work on mastering the overwhelming sensations I get in certain places, so I needn't run away. I'll try to come back tomorrow, if that's all right."

"You know it is. Come anytime."

When I returned home, I rested on the bed since my sleep was interrupted the night before. I dosed off. The next thing I knew, Alvin was leaning over me, grinning like he won a prize at the fair.

"You're cute when you sleep."

I laughed and sat up. Alvin perched beside me and brought our lips together.

The bank account!

The words were loud in my mind. I knew it was time to breach the subject, but his kisses were so sweet, and Alvin was in no hurry to stop. My arms went under his suit jacket to his suspenders. I followed the line to his waistband.

"Deb! You don't play fair when you try to tickle me."

"I remembered something, Alvin." I reached for my purse off the edge of the dresser. "I used some of the cash I had from my father to buy the dress last week and decided to put the rest of it into your account. At First National, I told them your name and address and turned over thirty dollars. They gave me a deposit slip, but I forgot about it."

I handed him the receipt and he took it with a look of bewilderment.

"I wanted to surprise you with a contribution, but when I finally looked at the balance they recorded…well, I think they might have put my money into the wrong account. Do we need to check with the bank about it?"

He glanced at the paper and slipped it into his pocket.

"I'll take care of it. And thank you for contributing. I know you wanted to get furniture for the sitting room, but you chose to think of me." His voice hitched and his embrace was complete tenderness. "It means a lot, Deb."

Alvin's reaction made no sense. He didn't deny the total, but he was moved by my tiny deposit in comparison.

At supper, Catherine spoke about attending a women's auxiliary meeting the following morning. Relishing the thought of not having to deal with her, my mind wandered to ways to make the most of my freedom. I could take more time in the kitchen, stretch out in the parlor, or lounge in the rose garden. I'd be the queen of the castle for a few hours.

My pleased smile must have stoked Alvin's interest. He excused us immediately after dessert and brought me to the bedroom where no concern other than our mutual passion stirred me that night.

The weightless lethargy of my sated body continued into the next morning, only managing basic toast and scrambled eggs for breakfast. Alvin was just as preoccupied with how we spent our night because he left without his lunch. I hid it in the icebox so Catherine wouldn't see it and set to work making a pie crust.

With Catherine gone, the cherry pie on the cooling rack, and Sabine busy polishing silver, I slipped upstairs. At the top of the flight, I turned to the right for the first time. The back hall seemed to go on forever as I went toward the door at the end.

Catherine's room was open. Stopping in the doorway, I peered inside. The red drapes on the windows gave it an eerie glow as the fabric rustled in the breeze, creating the illusion of a crimson pulse behind the closed curtains.

Vile.

I felt dirty just looking inside. When I touched the doorknob to pull the door shut, goosebumps bloomed up my arm. I shuddered and went to my room to prepare to bring Alvin his lunch. He had his break at eleven-thirty, and I wanted to be at the school several minutes before that so he wouldn't make alternative plans.

Boots on and purse in hand, I went to the kitchen to make a sandwich for myself should Alvin wish to eat together. I loaded his metal lunchbox and my reticule and food into a handbasket I found in the pantry.

I was soon on Government Street, where I caught a streetcar. Riding it downtown and around back westbound on the north side of the busy street, I disembarked at the corner nearest Barton Academy.

The gleaming white building and its towering cupola were as impressive as they had been when Alvin and I went exploring our first weekend in town. The shadows were still there too, though they could have been students in the upper windows this time. The open gates welcomed me to enter like a trap. Dozens of girls were in the yard, talking and eating. White shirtwaists were the main fair along with a multitude of solid colors for their ankle-length skirts.

When I stepped through the black gates, a wave of despair washed over me as powerful as the one that struck me at the cathedral. Then the flickers came.

Blood.

Illness.

Despair.

I went to my knees, dropping my basket as the cries echoed in my head.

A group of girls approached me. "May we help you?"

I nodded, trying to steady my nerves before speaking so my voice wouldn't waver. "I need to get outside the gates. Please."

"Go get the nurse, Hannah," one of them said while two others went to either side of me, hauling me to my feet.

"I've never seen her before, have you?" one whispered.

"She has a wedding band," the student carrying my basket replied.

I staggered between the girls, a hand reaching for the iron gate as soon as I could touch it. Breathing deeply in relief, I leaned against the outside of the fence.

"Thank you—all of you. Just set down my basket. I'll be all right in a moment."

A fourth girl ran to us, a woman of about forty-years-old in a nurse's uniform following.

"What happened?" the nurse asked.

"She nearly fainted, Nurse Wallace," one of the girls said as she motioned to me.

"You do look a tad pale, my dear. Who is your homeroom teacher?"

"I'm not a student. I came to bring my husband his lunch. If someone could send word to Alvin Farley, I'd appreciate it."

"Mr. Farley!"

"I told you he was married," another student said.

Nurse Wallace looked to them with a smile. "Go on, all of you run along. Hannah, you have my permission to wait outside Mr. Farley's door until the bell. He's on the third floor."

"She gets to go to the boy's corridor?" a brunette whined.

"It's not fair!" chimed another.

"No complaints, girls. The bell will ring in a moment. Run along before Principal Gentry thinks you're up to something. Now, Mrs. Farley," the nurse said when we were alone, "tell me what happened."

"I was overcome for a moment. It's nothing to be concerned about. The heat must have gotten to me, but I'm fine now. Thank you."

"I hope you don't think badly of the girls. As you can imagine, such a young and handsome teacher as Mr. Farley has captured their attention."

"Of course." I managed a smile.

The clanging of the bell denoting the end of the period rang out. The students in the yard picked up their belongings and went for the door.

"Would you like to come to my office?"

"No, thank you. I'll wait for Alvin here. You may go in if you need to. I'll be fine."

The nurse nodded and shifted to the front walk. She wanted to stay and observe my meeting with Alvin, but I didn't want her nosing into our conversation. I picked up my basket to prove I had strength and dexterity.

Then Alvin ran out the front door, a group of curious boys behind him.

"Deborah!" He took me by the arm. "What on earth—"

"You forgot your lunch."

"Yes, but the girl said you'd fallen."

"I was only momentarily weak. I'm fine now, Alvin."

Arm around my shoulders, he took the basket with his free hand and looked to the nurse standing a few feet away. "Thank you, Nurse Wallace."

"I'm happy to help, Mr. Farley." She walked slowly back to the building.

"Did you bring enough for yourself? We could picnic in my room. I've wanted to show it to you. Maybe I could even sneak you up to the cupola. I have forty minutes to spare."

"I don't know if I should."

"You must, Deb." He held a touch of pleading in his gaze. "It would be silly to come all this way and not see where I work."

The urge to bring him joy tugged on my heart. Could I risk utter collapse to please him? Was it possible to keep the spirits at bay and control my gift? I had told Althea I needed to put my studying into action, but faced with the reality of it, it terrified me.

Trying to bring lightness to the situation, I smiled. "Only if you promise me two things."

"What are those?"

"Keep beside me and kiss me thoroughly once we have privacy."

Smiling, Alvin tucked my arm around his. "Gladly, Deb."

Concentrating on completely grounding myself in the moment, we made our way past the starring eyes and through the unseen despair. Alvin paused to make a few introductions to the staff we passed, and then we were in the stairwell.

The echo of boots from the previous century mixed with the laughter of the boys headed outside for their break.

Once we were up a flight, one of the students called out "Mr. Farley's got himself a girl!"

A few whistles accompanied the words.

Alvin's rumble of laughter further chased the despair from me, even with the shadows following us up the next flight.

"Was this building always a school?" I asked as he led me down the corridor, empty of students.

"It was Alabama's first public school nearly a century ago, but the building was used as a hospital during the War Between the States."

So the soldier standing in the corner of Alvin's classroom with a crutch under one arm was completely normal.

Alvin set the basket on his desk and looked expectantly at me. "What do you think, Deb?"

It was similar to what he had at my father's school, but the look of ownership was new. "It's terrific, Alvin."

"Come see the view. It's rooftops, church spires, and blue skies all the way toward the river." Standing behind me at the open window, Alvin's arms went around my middle, and he kissed my neck. "I'm glad I forgot my lunch this morning."

His love momentarily drowned the discomfort coming from the soldier. I relaxed against him, trying to absorb his peace.

"Mr. Farley, a moment of your time."

Alvin stiffened, and then quickly released me as he turned to the harsh voice at the door.

"Principal Gentry, hello. May I introduce my wife to you?" I followed Alvin's lead up the aisle between the wooden desks to the pompous man who tried to hide his thinning mane by combing his hair the wrong way over his head. "I forgot my lunch this morning, and Deborah was kind enough to bring it to me."

"That's why I'm paying you this visit. Mrs. Farley seems to have caused a stir in her short time here. And seeing your display together, I don't doubt it."

I suppressed a shiver—not only from his coldness but the lingering vibrations of an ill-lived life. The principal might be more cause for concern than the ghosts.

Before I could open my mouth, Alvin stepped in front of me. Worry over me handling the situation much like I did with Aunt Catherine probably spurred him to visibly block me, but perhaps it was an instinctive maneuver to protect me from his boss.

"My apologies, Principal Gentry, but there are no students on this floor right now."

"Students or not, the moral code must be kept, as I'm sure you agree with me."

"Yes, sir."

"Good." He straightened. "I noticed there were several items in your mailbox in the office. You should collect them during your break."

"Thank you, sir."

The principal's gaze cut toward me before he left.

"If you want to collect your messages," I told Alvin, "I'll arrange our luncheon."

"Thanks, Deb. I'll be back in a few minutes."

Alvin's desk was within a few feet of the dejected specter in a Union uniform. I knew from my studies of Kardec that haunted places were filled with the lesser spirits—those who didn't know better or evil ones set upon mischief. This soldier looked lost.

When I paused for the basket, I looked into his haunted eyes. "It must be lonely, being so far from home. Your family is waiting for you, sir."

Images of a seaside New England village filtered through my mind followed by a wave of fear.

"There's no need to tarry here when your heart is elsewhere. I'm sorry you had to die in enemy territory, but we're on the same side now."

Visitors.

Bring me home.

"They won't come. You need to go to them. You'll be fine. Look for the light."

The arm not supporting his crutch raised, a finger pointing to the far wall that burned with a hazy yellow glow.

"Yes, there it is. Go to it."

He glided through the desks, pausing once to look back at me. All the sorrow he'd carried for nearly half a century spilt into my soul. I offered a smile and waved goodbye as a tear streaked my cheek. When he disappeared through the luminous wall, I was bereft with emptiness.

Silence.

I laughed aloud, believing I finally had a hold on my gift—that I could assist the spirits. And, most importantly, that I could help Sean by sending Eliza away.

Ten

When I left Barton Academy after a lovely picnic with Alvin, rather than riding the streetcar, I walked toward Rapier Avenue to expel my energy. I stopped at the house long enough to drop my basket on the front porch, then continued down the street.

Althea answered my rapid knock with wide eyes, then a smile.

"I thought the neighborhood was on fire with all that racket."

Laughing, I took her hand. "I did it!"

"You know better than that, child." She brushed off my touch and looked up and down the street before waving me over the threshold. "You can't be friendly like that where neighbors might catch you."

"I see your soul, not your skin, but I'm sorry if I made you uncomfortable."

Althea put an arm around me to steer me to the kitchen. "Now what has you so excited, Deborah?"

While she brewed coffee, I told her about my feelings at the school and the solider in Alvin's classroom.

"And he never came back?" she asked as she set the coffee and cookies on the table, taking the seat across from me.

"No, and I didn't feel anything until Alvin walked me to the entrance, but I was able to mask my discomfort and didn't get physically weak."

"So now you think you can take on Eliza Melling?"

"I believe I could."

"A lonely soldier is a lot different than a headstrong lover."

"You make her sound ominous." I stirred my coffee. "Sean is so kind, I don't see how he could be in love with anyone who wasn't the same."

Althea laughed. "So you and Alvin are exactly alike, are you?"

Smiling, I shrugged. "No, but neither of us are dangerous."

"Some might consider you exactly that with your gift." Her dark eyes flashed with warning. "Sean Francis has the heart of an explorer. He likes to discover new people and challenges. Yes, he's generous and loving, but he enjoys the acts for how they enrich his life. Take you, for example. You have something he wants."

"What's that?" I nibbled a shortbread cookie as I listened.

"Sean Francis felt the pull of an adventure when you shared your gift with him. He's catering to you with books and information because he wants to keep you close so when you dip into the unknown he has a box seat as the performance plays out."

"I can't believe that." The words were spoken automatically.

"Can't you, child?" She drummed the table with her fingers. "You've animated him like I haven't seen in years. He hasn't cast his heart to you, but his whole soul. The possibilities of reaching the spirit world through you have him mesmerized. I fear he'll push you too far, that you'll stretch beyond your abilities to please him, and be damaged in the process."

"That's impossible. Except for feeling weak, which passes, I've never been physically touched by the phenomenon."

Althea shook her head. "I know you've seen Eliza's stubbornness and jealousy flare."

"I can be just as stubborn. I'm the same age, and have energy to withstand her games."

"But you have a pure heart, child." Althea's hand patted mine. "Eliza, God rest her soul, could be as ruthless as her father and as biting as her mother. Sean was blinded by her allure. He happily followed her lead for the chance of another rush, whether from shirking the rules or with the pinnacle of love making."

"Were they intimate often?" I gripped my cup, waiting for a reply.

"Those last few months, she had him running ragged, seeking new times and locations where they could join without her parents finding out. He had to be creative because Mrs. Melling kept a close guard on Eliza. But the tighter she held her daughter, the more she rebelled." Althea stared at me with conviction. "If you try to force her into something, Eliza will fight back, and there won't be anything pretty about that."

The clock on the wall ticked the seconds. Steam rose from the coffee between us. The wind rustled the curtains through the open window.

"I have to try," I finally said.

"I know, child. And Sean Francis is counting on it, but please be careful."

After reading another chapter in the library, I silently made my way upstairs to study Eliza's art. Hoping to find a clue in the painting, I stood before the hearth and gazed at the expanse of flawless skin and raven hair. Her violet-blue eyes beckoned the viewer closer until you could feel her sensuous arms around you as she held you to her heaving bosom.

I crossed to the sketches, looking on them in a way I hadn't been able to do the night we'd been given the tour. The sense of movement in the languid poses was just as hypnotizing as the painting, though they lacked the depth of color—all but one that is. The full nude had her eyes colored that starling hue, while the torso and bust sketches were raw with passion and talent. They were done quickly compared to the full-body one within its mirrored reflection. The self-contemplation required for the detailed sketch depicted in a looking glass invited the viewer to linger as well. She was feminine in the extreme with the curves of her body and the dip of her waist. It must have been created by hours in a wasp-waist corset that were all the rage half a decade ago.

Do you like what you see? Sean surely did. Fortunately for me, he did more than look. Does that shock you?

Eliza's invisible touch outlined my shoulders. Unable to move, I continued to stare at her likeness.

You have an interesting figure. Half-woman, half-child. Married but still naïve. I wish I could draw you. Would you disrobe for me so I could capture all your glory for your virile husband?

Thinking what Alvin would do if he were to see a sketch of me like one of these, I shivered.

Eliza laughed. *Thrilling, isn't it? There's no other feeling like having sexual power over a man. I still wield that over Sean. Ask him what he does while looking at these sketches.*

"Deborah, what are you doing in here?" The shock in Sean's voice made guilt bloom across my face.

Turning to him, I saw Eliza fully formed beside him. She glimmered in a Regency era gown that accented her breasts.

"I wanted to look at Eliza's art in an attempt to better understand her." I crossed the room, expecting her spirit to move away, but she held her position by Sean.

"Did it work?"

I nodded, looking at her rather than Sean.

He followed my gaze. "Is she here?"

"Yes, in a gorgeous Regency gown. It's splendid."

"Mother Mary, help me." Sean bit his lip, crossed himself, and moved to the bed, perching on the edge of it, facing the sketches. "That was her Halloween costume five years ago. She was luscious."

"But why would she wear that?"

"For you to remind me—as if I'd ever forget. Our first time sharing ourselves fully happened in this room that night. I removed every stitch from her."

"That might be why I see her so clearly now—because an event so full of life happened in this room. She says your last time was here as well."

Sean's golden eyes were merry. "I'll always love you, Eliza, but don't tell all our secrets to Deborah. Can you hear me?"

"She nodded and is trying to lick your ear," I said.

He chucked and looked to me with his hooded eyes and an intimate smile. "I've got to get you out of here, Deborah. Alvin would bust my face if he knew we were in my bedroom together."

"Alvin doesn't have a violent bone in his body."

"Every man who plays football does, and he shared a few things with me the other night."

"Like what?" I asked as he took my arm.

"You know I'll not disclose our drinking secrets." Sean winked and started for the stairs.

Althea watched us descend, a kitchen towel wound tight in her hands.

"Don't frown at me, Althea," Sean said when we reached the hall. "I wasn't expecting to find Deborah in my bedroom."

"You both deserve thrashings."

"Nonsense," Sean said with a tone of dismissal. "Deborah's heart was in the right place even if her body wasn't. Besides which, Eliza was chaperoning."

She snapped the towel against Sean's backside before stalking towards the kitchen.

"Thank you, Althea," he said with a laugh. "Once again, I see the error of my ways!"

She turned back, finger pointing at him. "Then you'll see that Mr. Farley is fully informed of the working situation between you and Deborah, and you'll not be alone with her again."

Sean's hands went up in a plea of innocence. "Am I truly such a naughty boy, Miss Althea?"

She gave him a deadly stare before speaking. "Shall I go ask Miss Merritt her opinion on that, Sean Francis?"

"That was half a lifetime ago!" The incredulous tone was weakened by his guilty blush.

Althea pointed to me. "I'll not see you sully this child's name or endanger her relationship with her husband."

"Nor would I ever want to do such things."

"What is planned and what happens are two different kettles of fish, Sean Francis." Althea disappeared into the kitchen.

He turned to me, uncertainty on his face.

"I need to tell Alvin about my gift," I whispered.

Sean nodded and took my hand. "Take your time. Eliza won't leave me, will she?"

I smiled. "I doubt it. I did have a breakthrough today at Barton Academy. Ask Althea to tell you. I'll go home now—with the book."

He squeezed my hand before letting go. "Come for supper on Saturday with Alvin. Bring his aunt if you must."

I nodded and made my escape.

It was close to five before Alvin came home. He kissed me while I paused my knitting.

He looked around the room. "I want a chair here by yours. Shall we shop for one Saturday morning?"

"That sounds nice. We have a supper invitation that night to Sean's house. He said we could invite Catherine if we wanted."

"But you don't, do you?" The jut of his chin was defiant, a lopsided smirk on his lips.

"Of course not, but if you think it would be best, we will."

"I don't think I could tolerate their quips all evening."

"Let him know so he can arrange for another guest."

"I'll telephone him now."

Alvin left the room without noticing the Kardec book on my side table. I set my knitting on top of it and walked the space between my chair and the bookcase on the far wall, imagining a small couch there.

"He's going to see about getting one of the football players over." Alvin hugged me. "Will you be bored with that?"

"You men have fun with whatever conversations strike your fancy." I kissed him, lingering my lips on his as he pulled me closer. "As long as I'm with you, Alvin, I'm happy."

At supper, Catherine was in a worse mood than usual. She was so upset, she didn't speak—not even to Alvin—for the first ten minutes. She brooded in a yellow cocoon at her end of the table.

"I suppose," she finally said, "that I'll have to find something to entertain myself on Saturday since you're not taking any meals with me."

Eyes widening, I looked to Alvin.

He glanced from me to his aunt. "Deborah and I need a day together."

A whole day! I smiled at Alvin as I placed my hand on his knee.

"I suppose you're going to waste your money gallivanting around town on a wild spree."

"It's none of your worry," he said as the color rose to his face, "but I'm not in the least concerned with Deborah's spending habits, nor my own."

"Oh, everything is ruined." Her fork clattered to her plate. "Tessa! Tessa, I'm through. Take it all away!"

Tessa, Alvin, and I watched Catherine stalk from the room. Her heels clicked up the wood stairs and across the upper hall before her bedroom door slammed.

The cook gave a timid smile, to which I giggled.

"She's had a difficult year," Alvin murmured.

"And it's probably all her doing," Tessa declared before going back to the kitchen.

Alvin shrugged. "Now what do we do?"

"Enjoy a pleasant supper and dessert while you tell me all about our Saturday plans."

Eleven

Saturday morning, Alvin and I took the streetcar downtown. We enjoyed breakfast at a restaurant inside the Cawthon Hotel—which Alvin informed me was good, but not better than my own cooking—and then went window shopping until we found stores selling furniture. After much discussion, we settled on a small, tufted, blue couch big enough for Alvin to sit and prop his feet on, or for me to snuggle beside him, which I looked forward to doing as the nights chilled. He paid with a bank check, and then had me lead the way to Mademoiselle Bisset's shop.

"I want you to have another new dress or two, Deborah. You're always pretty, but it's nice to see you dressed up."

"Am I to be your trophy at supper tonight?" I teased.

"I have no problem dining with bachelors with my lovely wife."

Mademoiselle Bisset's store was bustling with Saturday shoppers, but she recognized me at once.

"Welcome Mrs. Farley—and Mr. Farley! My dear, you are lucky to have brought this one to town after the nuptials and not before, for he would have been snatched up in no time." She offered her hand to Alvin. "I am glad to meet you, Mr. Farley. May I trust that you found your wife the loveliest creature in the gown she purchased the other week and wish to buy her more?"

He adjusted his poke collar, looked around at the watchful eyes of shoppers and shop girls alike before smiling at Mademoiselle Bisset. "Yes, you're exactly right."

"There is no better compliment than a happy husband, Mr. Farley. Now, what will your wife need today?"

"Whatever she wishes, so long as it includes at least one evening gown and an outfit appropriate for Sundays."

We left an hour later. The dresses, sleepwear, and undergarments would be delivered to the house that afternoon.

"We have time to eat dinner before the couch and clothing are delivered," Alvin said. "Does seafood sound good?"

I agreed and we headed east, seeking a restaurant near the river Sean had recommended.

Once at a corner table away from the bustle of the kitchen noises, we sipped iced tea.

I took Alvin's hand. "Why are you spending so much money today?"

"Because you deserve to be spoiled, Deb." His thumb caressed the side of my palm. "Don't think I haven't noticed the way you rise early to cook my breakfast, not to mention those tasty desserts and my lunches. You've been patient with our living arrangement and the dearest thing to me these past weeks. But please don't worry about money."

"Was that deposit receipt balance correct?"

He nodded.

"I love you no matter what's in your account, but why didn't you tell me, Alvin?"

He dropped my hand when the waiter delivered our food, then thanked him. "Eat while it's fresh, Deborah."

The unspoken words festered between us, but I couldn't be upset with him when I was sitting on the truth of what I now knew was mediumship. If he told me about his money, I would tell him about my gift—sometime.

The softshell crab dipped in melted butter was excellent, the cornbread and greens as well. We ate without speaking, but we looked often to each other. Alvin ordered himself another crab when the waiter stopped to check on us, but I declined anything more.

"Uncle Jerald," he told me, "was in insurance and had his life insured for fifty thousand dollars. I received eighty percent of it when he died."

"Shouldn't the majority have gone to Catherine?"

"Or to their children, but in over five years of marriage, he and Catherine never had any, much to his disappointment. Cathy received ten thousand, but the original plan was for her to get it all. Uncle Jerald changed it last winter, and I don't think he told her because she was upset when his lawyer went over the papers before her, my mother, and me after the funeral. Maybe Uncle Jerald wanted it left to the next generation. I was his only nephew and named after him—Jerald Alvin Snodgrass."

"Or maybe he didn't love her anymore. She is rather difficult to live with."

"Deb." Alvin shook his head.

His second crab arrived, and he ate without looking at me.

"Alvin, I'm just trying to understand."

"There's nothing to understand. He changed the main beneficiary, and we'll never know why because Uncle Jerald is dead."

"But I could try—" I stopped before blurting my idea of seeking a connection with Uncle Jerald's spirit.

"You're doing more than enough at home, Deborah, and I appreciate it."

Guilt crept in because I wasn't doing all I could—at least not where Catherine was concerned. It was too difficult to play nice with her. "But why are we living with Aunt Catherine when you have the means of securing our own home?"

"Are you so unhappy there?"

The sadness in his eyes was palpable, and I couldn't drive the knife deeper when he had shared the truth with me. "You come home to me every day, and we're together each night. That's what I need, not a fancy house—just a room or two to call our own. And we have that, Alvin."

"I'm glad to hear that, Deb. The house is mine, but it doesn't feel right to kick Cathy out while she's in mourning."

"Then why does she act like I'm trying to take over her house when it doesn't belong to her?"

"She's still trying to work through her grief. I'll encourage her to look for a fresh start next spring."

"Next spring?" Anger threatened to boil over. "I'm supposed to put up with her pointed remarks another six months?"

Alvin shrugged. "I don't want to push her out when she's already lost Uncle Jerald."

"Why didn't you tell me all this before we came?"

His lips pressed into a straight line for a moment. "I didn't tell you about the inheritance because when I was in college…there was a girl."

"Yes?" I took his hand as gently as I said the word.

"I was in love with her. She came to every home game and we studied together. We'd meet wherever we could for a little alone time, and…well, I wanted to marry her. The day before I planned to propose, she found out I was at the university on scholarship and demanded to know what my father did. When she learned he worked in a Sloss furnace, she dropped me."

I watched his chin quiver as he fought back his emotions a moment.

"You mentioned to me about losing my uncle, and I still don't know how you found out because I only told the school I had a family emergency when I came down for the funeral. I was worried you somehow knew I'd come into money and your increased attentions were a young lady looking to keep her easy lifestyle."

"Alvin, I hope you realize I'm not like that."

"I came to understand you better when we started taking those walks this summer, but I was still nervous."

"It pains me that your heart was broken."

"You've healed it, Deb." Alvin's hand was on my cheek before his mouth went to mine in a quick—but public—kiss.

***

At six o'clock that evening, Alvin lounged on the new sofa while I dressed for supper in the bedroom. My sapphire gown from Mademoiselle Bisset's was silk and the orange sash a bold contrast to show off a perfect hourglass shape I didn't realize I had until acquiring the French shapewear.

Once my hair was piled on top of my head and the dangling crystal earrings hung from my lobes, I opened the door to the sitting room. Alvin set down the book he was reading and smiled with complete devotion as he crossed to me.

"Are you truly mine, Deb?" He kissed my throat and down toward the square neckline of the gown.

"Completely yours, Alvin Farley."

He started us in a box step, to which I followed his lead. "I'm claiming the first dance now so Sean or his guest can't take that from me."

"No matter who dances with me, it's you I love."

His smile and the mischievous twinkle in his eyes helped me see the young man he must have been in college with all his dreams within reach, from career to love. Hopefully he knew he had all that now, even if I wasn't part of his original plan.

Alvin excused himself to change into the tuxedo that had been delivered that afternoon. He had stopped after work the other day to have one fitted as a surprise. Not having seen him in a tuxedo before, I anxiously waited until he returned to the room.

"You're handsomer than ever, Alvin." My hands skimmed his jewel-toned blue bowtie he'd purchased from Mademoiselle Bisset, then over his shoulders. "The fit is perfection. I'd be happy staying here and looking at you all evening."

"I want to do more than look at you, Deb." The fire in his eyes and the sensual rumble of his voice had my arms about him in a second.

As our kiss continued, I caressed over the fine weave of his clothes, feeling the man within in a new light.

Cling to Alvin, for she will try to kill him.

The masculine voice was loud in my head, causing me to jerk back from Alvin's loving embrace. A shimmer flicked near the closed door, tall and sturdy like a man. Then it was gone.

"What is it, Deb?" The concern on Alvin's face combined with the thought of losing him nearly brought tears to my eyes.

"A flight of fancy, I suppose." I mustered a smile and took his hand. "When do we leave?"

We descended to the first floor. Catherine stared at Alvin from her chair in the parlor as she always did—with lust.

"What do you think, Cathy?" he asked with complete confidence.

"You've outdone yourself with all the purchases this week. Deborah is beautiful, and you're handsome beside her, Alvin. Would you like a drink before you go? I brewed tea that's been chilling."

She'll make you a widow, too.

I clung to Alvin's hand. Thinking I was urging him to leave, he said goodbye to his aunt and we went down the front steps, freeing us from potential harm.

As we approached Sean's house, the strains of a ragtime piano tune floated out the open windows with more clarity than a typical recording. Alvin's pace quickened to the front door where he knocked loudly to be heard over the music. The sound stopped abruptly.

Sean answered the door, utterly dashing in a tuxedo with a white bowtie. "Come in, my favorite new friends."

"Thank you, Sean," Alvin said as he motioned me ahead of him through the narrow entry.

The door closed and when I turned to our host, he was taking in the sight of us under his electric chandelier.

"It should be criminal to look as well as you do together." Sean lifted my hand to his lips. "You grow lovelier each time I see you, Deborah. Marriage to Alvin is maturing you impeccably, and Alvin is wearing his joy like a peacock with that dash of color at his throat and the smile of a satisfied man."

We grinned and blushed as we followed him into the parlor where Eliza materialized enough to glare at me from the corner with the piano.

This could have been my life.

"Was that you playing when we knocked?" I asked Sean, ignoring Eliza.

"It was. Do either of you sing?"

"Only in a large congregation when no one can hear me," I replied.

Alvin shook his head. "We weren't much of a church-going family."

Sean turned on him. "And yet you turned out well. How is that? If I didn't attend Mass and the confessional regularly, I'd be in Hell by now."

"So you'd still believe even if you didn't attend?" Alvin countered.

"Believe it or not, there's a force greater than you and me up there, and spirits are all around us."

Sean's pointed remark startled me, but I knew he was testing if I'd shared my gift with Alvin. I shook my head, and he frowned.

"Do you believe in angels or ghost?" Sean asked Alvin.

"Only the angel I was fortunate enough to marry." He kissed my cheek.

Sean's huge grin revealed both his chipped tooth and the fact he'd forgiven me for staying silent with Alvin. He answered the front door and returned with Chuck Brady—the young man with long sideburns who had brought Sean to the cathedral when I was weak. Chuck was boisterous and fun, but I could tell he was getting on Alvin's nerves from his constant attempts to engage me with banter over the pre-supper drinks.

"Chuck," Sean said in a tone to get the younger man's attention, "if you don't stop flirting with Deborah, her husband will make sure you're on the other football team as an excuse to smash your face into the ground."

"He's too nice a guy to do something like that," Chuck declared.

Alvin slung back a whisky. Then he threw Chuck over his shoulder with one arm before setting him roughly back on his feet. "Don't test me."

As soon as Althea struck the supper gong, Sean was at my side to escort me. Alvin and I were on the long sides of the table and Sean and Chuck at the head and foot. Althea brought in the first platter as soon as Sean had prayed.

The men kept up a steady conversation about the football game next Saturday, while Eliza, faded to a near-shapeless shadow, hovered near the sideboard.

When she brought in the cheesecake, Althea gave each of the men a stare. "Y'all be kind to Miss Deborah and allow her to choose the topic over dessert. It's been one football story after another in here. I don't see how she's tolerated it."

"You should have invited a few debs, Spunner," Chuck said.

"I'm too old to be acquainted with all the debutants."

"I could have helped you. Sadie Marley is on the next block and would have been easy enough to engage, you being friends with her sister's husband and all."

"I'd never hear the end of it from John if I invited his sister-in-law to supper. He teases me enough as it is when his wife tries to match me with her at their parties." Sean poured fresh champagne. "What do you wish to speak of, Deborah?"

"The infernal obsession men have with football," I replied with a straight face.

They all laughed, and Alvin stretched his arm across the table to me. I offered my hand, and he entwined our fingers a few moments.

"Are you coming to cheer us on next week?" Chuck asked me.

"I wouldn't miss seeing Alvin play for anything."

We finished dessert and moved into the library. Sean lit a pipe and offered cigars to the others. I settled on the chaise and watched Alvin prepare the chessboard.

"Who is going to play me?" he asked.

"I'll give it a go," Chuck took the seat opposite, giving Sean the opening to join me on the chaise.

Sean lowered his pipe. "Are you enjoying yourself?"

"Very much, except for the fact that Eliza is often manifesting herself to make sure I can see her giving me the evil eye."

His head went back with his laugh, turning the others' attentions.

"And how is cozying up to Deborah any better than what you got onto me about before supper?" Chuck asked Sean.

"It's my job as host to pay each guest special attention."

"Then come sit on my lap and whisper sweet nothings in my ear, Spunner."

Alvin playfully slugged Chuck on the shoulder. "Don't be obtuse, Brady."

Eliza's form flickered closer. Seeing my eyes move to the space between our seat and the chess game, Sean dropped his voice.

"What is she doing?"

"Making a lewd gesture, if you must know."

Sean stifled a chuckle, then whispered. "Althea told me about your experience at Barton. That's very promising. If I can get rid of Chuck, will you help Eliza tonight?"

I closed my eyes, refusing to look at Sean's pleading gaze or the shadow of his fiancée.

"Checkmate!" Alvin roared.

"What? We barely started," Chuck said with incredulousness. "I demand a redo."

As they reset the board, Sean took my hand. "Please, Deborah."

He's mine!

I nodded.

"Have you finished the book?"

"Not yet. It's a lot to digest, and I don't read when Alvin is home. I like to be able to talk to him."

"Having a spouse with you in the evenings must be a great comfort."

"It's the best feeling in the world." I looked into his golden eyes. "I want to help you clear your life so you can have that too."

Sean's return gaze was intense.

If you weren't married, he'd have a hand under your skirt while tonguing your décolletage by now. He does love a good pair and yours are set off wonderfully tonight.

My hand went to my chest, and I felt the color drain from my face.

"What is it?" Sean rested a hand on my knee, but I jerked to my feet.

Chuck raised his head from the game. "Did Spunner get fresh with you?"

"He knows better than to try something with Deborah," Alvin said without looking up while moving one of his pieces. "It's your turn."

The young man made his move, then Alvin closed the game on his turn.

Chuck groaned. "I'm not one to go in for a third beating." Turning to our host who now stood beside me, he questioned. "Will there be dancing tonight?"

Sean glanced at my stiff posture. "I'll not put Deborah through the challenge of three men on her lone dance card."

"Then I'll be off. Next time make the numbers even, Spunner."

"I'll try, Chuck. Thank you for joining us."

We said our goodbyes and found ourselves in the front hall after the door closed.

Alvin's hand was wrapped around mine, and I leaned my shoulder against his firm arm. Looking down at me, he smiled before kissing me.

If you want him to take you, Sean and I would happily watch.

I flinched as though stung by the vulgar words.

"What—" Alvin started but I turned on Sean.

"How could you love someone like that? She's crude and the most ill-mannered soul, alive or dead, I've ever met!"

Sean gave a sheepish grin. "She was full of excitement."

"What is going on?" Alvin took me by the shoulders. "Who are you talking about?"

"Eliza Melling, Sean's dead fiancée." I broke from the grip and went for the stairs where she waited. "Do you hear that, Eliza? You're dead. Dead and you should be gone! Why don't you leave?"

"Deborah, did you drink too much?" Alvin's touch was gentle as he turned me to him.

"I wish I had."

"That could be arranged," Sean offered.

Alvin tucked me to his side and turned to our host. "Thank you for supper, but I think I should bring Deborah home."

"Not yet," Sean said with conviction. "There's something Deborah needs to tell you."

Alvin's eyes widened with confusion. "What is he talking about, Deb?"

Sighing, I expelled the words. "I see and hear spirits."

He leaned away from me as though repulsed. "What spirits?"

"I don't know them all by name or even see all the ones I hear." I pointed to the bottom of the stairs. "But Eliza is right there, taunting me. She probably wants us to go back to Sean's room so we can look upon her nakedness."

"Deborah, I think you're a bit hysterical right now. It might be best if you don't say anything."

"I'm not hysterical, Alvin. I'm blazing mad!"

"You won't be able to do anything with your emotions flared," Sean warned. "Come relax for a few minutes."

As we passed into the parlor, I trembled with anger as my mind raced with the information from the Kardec book. There had to be something I could use to give me time, even if I hadn't tested it before.

When I figured it out, I turned back and pointed at Eliza. "In the name of the Lord, Jesus Christ, you will *not* enter this room!"

To my delight, she was abruptly stopped in the doorway by an unseen force. Eliza switching from detailed to shadowed form produced the same result.

I had created a barrier between the living and the dead!

Twelve

Laughing as Alvin sat beside me in the parlor, I watched Eliza fade away.

"What is she doing?" Sean asked as he took the chair across from us.

"My words stopped her from following, so she went upstairs."

"You can do that?" Power gleamed in Sean's eyes, making me think of Althea's warning.

"Apparently, but I haven't needed to make a barrier before." Hoping to cool his enthusiasm, I spoke more with a sober voice. "She's a horror, Sean. Eliza is doing nothing good for you by hanging around. Even if you can't see or hear her, she's putting out all sorts of energy, and it isn't remotely pure or helpful."

He lowered his eyes and nodded.

Alvin squeezed my hand, causing me to look at him. "Please explain what's going on, Deborah. It sounds like a bunch of nonsense."

"You told me you didn't know how I knew your uncle died. Well, when I saw you in the hall that day at the school, the words came to my mind."

"What words?"

"'His uncle died. Pray for him.'"

"You heard that?" Alvin asked.

"When I saw you, that impression came to my mind. I can't always tell if it's something I hear or words I see in my mind, but the messages come from beyond."

"Beyond what?"

"Beyond this life. There's so much more out there, Alvin. More than we'll ever know. Some people are sensitive to messages from the other side. Apparently, I'm one of them."

"She's a medium," Sean said. "An extremely gifted one."

Alvin crossed his arms.

"I never told you because I didn't think you'd understand," I said. "All my quirks, as you call them, are related to this second sight. I used to think it was something I had no control over, but Sean loaned me a book about it, and I'm learning more."

Alvin turned on Sean. "If you're feeding her with this nonsense—"

"No, Alvin, I've known since I was four that I heard and saw more than anyone else. The book is only helping me understand that I'm not alone and giving me instruction in how to better use the abilities I have."

"Who told you about my uncle and asked you to pray for me?"

"I'm not sure beyond it was the soul of someone who loved you." I paused, knowing I needed to speak now rather than withhold more information. "But I heard Uncle Jerald before we left the house this evening. He's concerned for your safety. He thinks Catherine will harm you."

Alvin shook his head. "I can't believe this."

"You must!" Sean sat forward. "Deborah couldn't go into the cathedral because she felt the weight of the dead from the graveyard that used to be there a hundred years ago—something she knew nothing about. She saw the ghost of a soldier in your classroom at Barton Academy and sent him home after nearly fifty years of waiting. And she can see my fiancée's antics wherever I go because Eliza is haunting me."

Alvin stood and paced the room. "I could use another drink, Spunner."

"Of course." Sean crossed to the decanters.

Alvin avoided eye contact with our host, but thanked him for the glass. They both took tumblers of Sean's favorite Irish whiskey in hand, and I joined them near the piano.

I gently touched Alvin's tuxedo sleeve. "I'd like to ask your uncle about why he changed the beneficiary in his insurance policy. You don't have to say anything right now—just think about it. I won't go seeking him, but if he communicates with me again like he did today, I want to use that connection."

"Capitalize on the link," Sean said. "That's a brilliant idea."

"I don't like the sound of that." Alvin's fists tightened.

"There are no benefits to reap, Alvin. The change was already done, it's just a way to understand why, especially since he's worried about you—as am I. Don't answer me now, just think about it. I'll be busy enough tonight trying to handle Eliza."

"She was always a handful." Sean's smile drifted into memories, and he bit his lower lip.

"Since I can block her from a room," I told him, "I should be able to trap her in an object. Kardec mentioned similar situations in the book. Hopefully that will help you clear her from your mind so you can focus on the future rather than the past. What do you think?"

"It's worth a try."

I looked at Alvin. "And you?"

He shrugged. "It all sounds ludicrous to me."

"Could you make Eliza show herself to Alvin?" Sean asked. "That way he might believe us."

"I'd rather he had blind faith than knowledge." I left the words unspoken that Sean had believed me from the beginning.

When I turned away, Alvin reached for my arm. "Deb," he whispered. "I know you aren't a liar, but please understand that this all sounds like parlor tricks to me. I don't know what to think when you spout these foolish ideas."

A lump welled in my throat. "My life isn't foolish, Alvin."

I left the room before tears could streak my face. They fell as I climbed the stairs.

Men are ridiculous. Eliza said from the doorway to Sean's bedroom.

"Yes, they can be, Eliza." I followed her into the room and sat on the floor, motioning her shadow to me. "We're the same age, and I'm sure we have similar thoughts about many things though you appear to enjoy shocking me."

Some things are easy—and amusing.

"Is that why you're haunting Sean, because it's easy and amusing?"

Her shadow shimmered red, then materialized in an opaque splendor of her true shape.

Don't tell him, but I was unfaithful in life. As penance, I'm trying to be faithful in death. Besides, he needs me.

"What he needs is a woman by his side to hold him at the end of each day."

He needs it more than once a day. Eliza smiled. *Sean was the best lover. And he never made me cry like your husband has to you.*

"Alvin doesn't understand this side of me. He's all about mathematical formulas, and you can't explain spirits with an algebraic equation."

I'll give him something he can't deny.

"I want Alvin to believe in me without knowing."

Men are too dense for that. Sean and the deacon never saw what was right under their noses. You might want to relax, Deborah, because this could hurt.

Eliza was there, physically pushing into me as I defended my body against a threat I'd never known. The mental strain of fighting to keep her out curled my limbs with excruciating pain as I tried to spiritually claw her away. I fell back on the rug as vibrations wracked my frame with my waning effort against her onslaught.

"No, Eliza! Please don't!" I managed to cry before losing control of my body.

The others thundered up the stairs and knelt beside me. Alvin grasped my hand and Sean held my other arm in an attempt to quiet my trembling body.

Alvin turned an accusing eye on Sean. "What have you done to her?"

"Nothing! You heard her call out Eliza's name, not mine."

Althea came to the doorway. "Is she all right?"

"We don't know," Sean answered.

My body stopped vibrating and my mouth opened. "I'm here, Sean."

The strange voice further washed me in panic.

"What?" Alvin brought a hand to my face. "You don't sound right, Deb."

The electric bulbs in the room burst, leaving us in a shadowed world of ambient light from the far off hall sconce. Althea shifted in the doorway, further lengthening the shadows.

Eliza turned my head toward Sean. "I would give anything to have one more ride on Flora with you along the Eastern Shore."

"Eliza, my kitten." Sean lowered his face to me.

Alvin knocked him onto his backside with a hard shove. "Don't touch my wife!"

"But it's Eliza—she's taken control of Deborah." He scrambled back to my side.

"Do not touch the vessel!" The voice from me commanded.

"Eliza?" Sean leaned close once more.

"Stay back!" Althea said from her post at the door. "You'll get that girl killed if you don't abide by the rules."

Sean sprang back a few feet, squatting on his haunches. Alvin followed suit on his side, eyes bulging with fear.

My mouth went slack. A continuous stream of greenish vapor curled from my parted lips. It rose to the ceiling as the others watched in horror and awe. The mass began to make the movements of a body of water, rippling as it lowered from the height of the room to float a couple feet above me.

Out of the smoke, a horse galloped around the captive audience.

On the mare's back, two figures took shape in remarkable detail despite the gaseous form. A man sat behind a woman, arms around her waist. As his features clarified into Sean's, his hands roamed the young woman's curves as their ride continued in an oval track above my still body.

"You were glorious, Eliza," Sean whispered.

The vapor dispersed then regathered before Sean in the life-sized, naked form of his fiancée. A hand reached out to him and he raised his to meet it.

"No, Sean Francis!" Althea snapped.

"To feel her one more time—"

As soon as his fingertips brushed through those of the figure's, the vapor swirled with tornadic fury and slammed into my abdomen. My body lurched. I groaned, and then doubled over.

"Deb, my love." Alvin cradled me in his arms as his eyes filled with unshed tears. "I'm sorry for doubting."

As my non-responsive state continued, Alvin's fear turned to anger as he held me. Petrified of the fury rising within Alvin's tense body, I was too spent to speak though I wanted nothing more than to calm him.

Glaring across the few feet that separated them, he glowered at Sean. "I'll kill you if she's damaged!"

Sean shook his head, unable to speak as his own emotions filled his chest. He crossed to the dresser, lighting the hurricane lamp kept there for emergencies.

Adjusting the wick so the oil didn't burn too bright, Sean carried it to Alvin.

"Would you like to lay her on my bed?"

"You must be daft, Spunner!"

"Perhaps," Althea said from the hall, "one of the guest rooms would be more appropriate."

"But I didn't mean—"

"Sean Francis," she said quietly but sternly, "why don't you give the Farleys a bit of space?"

Sean set the oil lamp on the nearby table and sulked while Althea led Alvin as he carried me across the hall to the purple guest room. She turned on a small table lamp.

"Do you wish a doctor called, Mr. Alvin?" Althea asked once he laid me on the soft bed.

"How would I explain what happened? I don't even know what I witnessed, but would you first help me remove the gown so she can rest more comfortably? That's okay, isn't it, Deb?"

His voice was exasperated, but he brushed a kiss on my cheek and gazed into my eyes. I managed to nod.

Heeled slippers and gown removed, Alvin took Althea's advice of removing the shapewear that was over my ecru chemise. I winced and grunted in a pain a few times, but welcomed the freedom once I was left in my underset.

"She seems tender in her belly, the poor child," Althea remarked as he lifted me while she turned down the bed.

"That's where that…that thing crashed into her."

"Shall I check her, Mr. Alvin?"

He nodded, stepped back a pace, and crossed his arms to hide the tremble in his limbs.

Althea lifted the hem of my camisole and gently pulled down the waistband of my panties, exposing an area of darkening bruises I could feel marring the pale skin around my naval. The housekeeper gasped and Alvin flung open the door.

"You bastard!"

I heard Alvin tackle Sean on the rug in the hall. Managing to barely lift my head, I witnessed Sean go down with his best defensive moves. They wrestled, neither bothering to speak. Althea covered me and went for the men outside the bedroom doorway.

"Sean Francis!" She pulled him by the collar. "That's no way to handle things at your age. And Mr. Alvin, I'd think you'd better watch over your wife, no matter what you think this man has done."

"He led Deborah into harm's way with that devilry!" Alvin said as he staggered to his feet.

"But she wouldn't want you to hurt him, no matter what happened. I know Miss Deborah well enough to believe that." Althea shook her head. "Sean Francis, you look a fright. I hope you're ashamed of yourself."

"Yeah." He wiped his bloody nose on the torn sleeve of his tuxedo jacket and pulled off the bowtie that was hanging from its final few inches before he stood. "But I couldn't let him pound me to a pulp."

"He's your guest, and his wife is hurt."

"She is?" Remorse filled his eyes. "I'm sorry, Alvin. Ectoplasm has the potential for damage when it reenters the body."

"She's burned and bruised where that thing struck her. If something you bring on hurts her again, nothing will stop me from thrashing you," Alvin stated before going for the bathroom to wash.

"I'd do anything to hold Eliza again," Sean lamented.

"Apparently," Althea replied, "that includes sacrificing your neighbor for the chance."

"I did no such thing. Deborah came here willingly."

"You swayed her, and you know it," Althea accused. "Her husband knows it too. I even warned her about it when I first met her."

"But she has the gift! Deborah has the potential to bring herself fame and fortune if used properly."

"She doesn't want to be used, Sean Francis. That girl just wants to be a good wife and build a loving home with her husband. She agreed to try to help you as a friend, not as a stepping stone to some greater plan." How she knew me on such a deep level, I didn't understand, but she pegged my wants with precision. Althea smoothed Sean's ruffled hair, not bothering to hide the heartache she felt over the situation.

"Don't look at me like that, Althea. You know I'd never purposely misuse someone. I just want to help Deborah reach her full potential."

"Not everyone is comfortable at high levels of performance, especially with something dangerous."

"Mediumship isn't—"

"You know it is, Sean Francis! Spiritually, mentally, emotionally, *and* physically dangerous." Althea shook her head. "Clean up the glass from the lightbulbs in your room while I get some water boiling in case she needs a hot drink."

They went their separate ways and then Alvin was back, his face still damp from washing.

"Deb, I'll stay with you." He kissed my forehead and sat beside me. "Rest if you can."

I managed to smile and squeezed his hand when he captured mine.

Thirteen

I woke with an ache in my middle and turned to try to relieve it, but winced with the effort.

"Don't move, Deb." Alvin's warm hand captured mine and brought it to his lips. He kissed my fingers as he shifted to sitting on the edge of the bed. "How do you feel?"

"Like someone wound my stomach too tight."

Alvin's tuxedo jacket was off and he wore a concerned expression on his square face. I tried to remember all of what had happened as I looked around the room, rich with royal purple and gold trim.

Gasping at the memory, I nearly lurched upright. "Eliza! She forced herself into me."

Alvin brought his hands to my shoulders. "I'm sorry I didn't believe you, Deb, but I didn't know such things were possible. It was frightful. I thought I'd lost you." His forehead dropped to mine, lips on my temple. "I never knew how much you meant to me until that moment. I loved you before, but now…"

He kissed down my neck, highlighting the fact that I was without clothes. I managed a smile as my hand trailed up his white shirt to the thickness of his upper arm. "Could I have something to drink?"

"Coffee or tea?"

"Either, but preferably tea. Thank you, Alvin."

"Don't try to move, Deb. I'll help you sit up when I return."

After he left, Sean hurried in. "I'm glad you're awake, darling. I had no idea Eliza was so formidable." He sighed with longing. "But you, Deborah, are gifted. Never in my lifetime will I meet another who's as sensitive a medium. Charlatans abound, but you're pure and powerful as a physical medium. The display of ectoplasm was beyond anything I could have hoped to witness."

"What are you doing in here?" The harshness in Alvin's voice was raw.

Fear whitened Sean's face as he looked between us. "I heard you leave, and I wanted to check on her."

"She's all right, no thanks to you. Althea is going to bring a tray. As soon as Deborah can walk, we'll go home."

"You could stay here," Sean offered. "Althea could sit with her while you collect what you need for the night. That would allow Deborah more time to rest."

"I don't know if that's a good idea," Alvin said.

"Please think of it as an option." Sean backed to the door. "And let me know if you need anything."

Alvin waited by the bedside until Althea arrived with a tray. She set it on the dresser and removed a red shawl she had over her arm.

"I brought this up, thinking you might want to cover your shoulders while you drink. I keep it here in case the weather changes before I go home."

"Thank you, Althea. I would like to use it."

Alvin helped me sit while she propped pillows behind me. Then the knitted shawl was draped around me, the coverlet folded to my waist, and I was pronounced well enough to partake of the chamomile tea.

"How do you feel, Deb?" Alvin asked.

"I'm tired and sore."

"Would you like to sleep here or go home?"

"I want to finish my work with Eliza before leaving, so it will best if we stay."

"I don't want you communicating with that devilish spirit again, Deb. It's dangerous."

"Now that I know what she's capable of, I'll be ready the next time."

"There wouldn't be a next time if it was up to me. You don't need to sacrifice yourself for Sean's dead fiancée. You're too precious to me, Deb. If you aren't up to the walk, Sean could drive us, and I'd carry you to and from the automobile."

"I really am tired, Alvin. Let's stay here. I won't seek out an altercation, but if the opportunity arises, I'll attempt to handle Eliza again. I know what to expect."

He frowned a moment, then stood. "I'll gather a nightgown, a dress for you to wear in the morning, brushes—"

"That's plenty for me, Alvin, but don't forget your own supplies."

He nodded. "I'll send Althea up on my way out."

Althea came into the room. "I'm sorry, child. Sean Francis doesn't see beyond his goal when he's set on something."

I nodded my understanding—I was warned after all. We sat in silence until Alvin returned with a travel case. He had changed out of his tuxedo and wore brown trousers and his old navy college blazer, which he removed after setting down the luggage.

Althea questioned him about any further needs, then promised to be back to cook breakfast in the morning before closing the door on her way out.

"Now, Deb, are you ready to try standing?"

Alvin looked upon me with such pure emotion it made me smile. "I believe so."

He watched over me as I brought my legs to the edge of the bed. "Sit for a minute in case lightheadedness overtakes you. I've seen men twice your size go down after an injury because they stood too quickly."

I laughed and held my hands to him. "I feel so connected to you right now, Alvin."

His grin created smile lines and flashed his straight teeth. "I don't know what it was I felt before now, but you're completely mine, Deborah Farley, and I hope I'm all yours."

I stood, wrapping my arms around his shoulders so I could kiss him. One of Alvin's hands slipped up my chemise so it lay warm and sensual on my bare back. Our mutual kisses continued until my legs weakened.

Alvin's attentions were precise and loving as I changed for bed. I was pleased he chose my newest blue silk nightgown from Mademoiselle Bisset's. He even had the forethought to bring my dressing robe, so I was covered when he escorted me to the bathroom.

"She's getting about fairly well," I heard him tell Sean while he waited for me in the hall.

"I'll leave my door open tonight," Sean replied. "Holler if you need anything."

Alvin closed our door and saw me into bed before changing into his pajamas. He spooned behind me, warm and strong.

"The change of scenery is nice," he whispered as he caressed my hip. "It makes me want to plan a getaway, especially since we didn't have much of a honeymoon. We could spend the weekend at a hotel across the bay this autumn. Then over Christmas, we could travel further after stopping to see our folks."

"I'd enjoy both of those things, Alvin."

Knowing he would never attempt to be intimate in Sean's house, I fell asleep without worrying about Eliza watching us.

***

I woke in darkness. Shifting in bed, I felt Alvin's bulk behind me. His breathing was even, a light snore rumbling every few seconds. As my eyes adjusted to the dark, I saw our open bedroom door. A faint glow beyond drew my attention. Slowly, I sat up, testing both my strength and Alvin's sleep.

Steady-footed and with Alvin still snoring, I walked to the doorway. Sean's room across the hall had a trail of light from the full moon through his open window. It beckoned me to enter. Or maybe it was the pull of Eliza. Her painting was radiant in the soft illumination as though challenging me to banish her. My bare feet stopped when I was before the mantel beneath her gaze.

You couldn't stay away. Not that I blame you. Sean and I have both been accused of being magnetic individuals.

"Eliza, show yourself." Knowing what I was up against embedded my words with power as I mentally prepared several of Kardec's ideas to call upon for protection.

She appeared at once, a misty figure in a dark riding habit. Noticing her heavy dress, she changed it for a nightgown in the twinkling of an eye.

I can't have you outshine me, can I?

"Whatever makes you feel good about yourself, Eliza, because this is your new home. You will not leave this room."

She scoffed and floated for the door. Blocked. She tried both a wall and window to the same effect.

You think you're clever, but this won't end the way you expect.

"Your games have gone on long enough. Sean needs space from you, and you need to move on."

Eliza's hand went to a hip defiantly. *How can I now that I'm trapped here?*

"I'll take care of that shortly."

If you try to push me around, I'll enter you again. All I need to do is throw your body on Sean's bed and call for Alvin. Your husband will be so upset, he'll kill Sean. Then I'll have Sean, and you'll be alone because your husband will be in prison.

I held my ground. "Cease your unholy plans, Eliza Melling."

Sean is watching you. He's feigning sleep, but through the fringe of his eyelashes he's studying the way the silk moves across your breasts and captures your thighs. I bet he's imagining kissing you in those places. He's talented with his tongue.

"Silence!" I shouted as I advanced.

Eliza opened her mouth, but nothing came out. Fury in her hollow eyes, she lunged.

Concentrating all my energy on being as insubstantial as she, Eliza fell through me to the ground.

"Deb!" Alvin ran into the room, but I couldn't turn to him.

"Give her space," Sean said as he stood from his bed. "She's communicating with Eliza."

I pointed, honing all my energy at the ghost. "You have no power over me, Eliza. Your haunting here is done. You will go into your painting and stay there quietly until you are ready to fulfill your personal penance through honesty. When you share the truth of your devious life, you will then move on."

You can't do this to me! Her words blazed in my mind like a lighted theater marquee.

"Watch me." Reaching for her, I circled Eliza until she was between me and the painting. "You will go into your painting!"

As I stepped forward, she stepped back. Behind me, Alvin came nearer, but I couldn't divert my attention. My arms and legs quivered, but I inched closer, trapping the spirit before the fireplace. Her silent scream unleashed a wind that plastered the nightgown against my body with the force of a hurricane.

"Accept your new place. Go into the painting." My hands brushed her cold form as I motioned her up. "Go, and prepare yourself to move on. Allow Sean peace."

She clawed at me, causing my teeth to chatter and gooseflesh to bloom across my arms as I worked to keep her at bay.

"E—E—Eliza, go!"

The energy leaving my spent body had me stumbling to the floor.

Then arms were around my middle, holding me upright against Alvin's broad chest.

"I've got you, Deb."

"Send Eliza Rose away," Sean said from beside us. "We're both here for you."

I allowed myself a moment to breathe deeply before speaking. "Eliza Rose Melling, I command you to go into the painting!"

The use of her full name embedded my words with more authority. The invisible tug-of-war hastened. I found myself pressed between the mantel and Alvin as I looked into the eyes of the self-portrait. The image above appeared to wink at me as Eliza's spirit disappeared into the framed space.

My legs gave out.

Catching me before I could fall, Alvin turned for the nearest chair. "Fetch her dressing robe, Sean."

I collapsed against Alvin's shoulder as soon as I was cradled in his lap.

His lips brushed my cheek. "Is she gone?"

"Yes," I whispered.

"I'm glad to have been there for you this time."

Sean returned with my robe, and Alvin tucked it around me.

"You did it, Deborah," Sean said. "There's so much good you can do to save others as you've saved me."

"I don't want to perform parlor tricks before an audience, Sean."

"You're too powerful to ever be mistaken for that."

"You're not to push her into anything," Alvin said with gruffness as he stood with me in his arms. "I'm glad she solved your haunting—or whatever that was—but she's been physically drained twice now. Her work here is done."

Fourteen

Sunday morning, I would have drug my feet rather than get dressed, but I knew Alvin was hungry, and Althea was sure to have a hearty breakfast waiting for us at eight.

Wearing the blue skirt and blouse Alvin had picked out for me, I watched him finagle the red bowtie that matched his suspenders as he looked in the dressing table mirror.

"Alvin, will we go home right after breakfast?" I hated to admit it, but I was foggy-headed and weak.

"Sean likes to go to Mass from what I can tell, so I don't want to hold him up. You can take a nap once we get home. You look a tad tired, but much better than I expected after what happened." Love and affection filled his gaze as his lips met mine.

"Will you stay with me when I rest?" I asked in between kisses.

He nodded and smiled. "For as long as you'd like, Deb."

Part of me felt guilty for enjoying the new attitude Alvin possessed. I had to remind myself that he had always loved me; this was just a magnification of those emotions. Besides, a little extra romance between spouses never hurt.

The gong sounded, calling us to the dining room. Alvin slipped on his jacket and we descended the stairs.

Sean stood by his chair at the head of the table and motioned to the seats on either side of him. "Good morning, Alvin and Deborah. I trust all was comfortable for you two the remainder of the night."

"Yes, thank you," Alvin said as he pushed in my chair.

Sean prayed over the food, and I thanked him when he poured me a cup of coffee.

Alvin and Sean chatted about the football game next Saturday, and Sean promised to give him word as soon as he knew the start time.

"We won't keep you," Alvin told Sean. "Deb is still tired, and I know you like to get to church, so I'll collect our things while she finishes eating."

Sean took my hand as soon as Alvin was on the stairs. "If I made an ass of myself last night, Deborah, I'm sorry. I never meant for you to get hurt."

I shook my head. "It's too fresh for me. I'm not thinking straight."

He gave a sheepish grin. "I'll try to be better, Deborah, and do my best to make things right between us."

I met Alvin at the foot of the stairs. He had my sapphire gown thrown over his shoulder and the bag in hand.

"I didn't want to cram it into the case," he explained.

I smiled at his thoughtfulness. "It looks lovely on you."

He laughed and turned to Sean. "Thank you for hosting us. And thank Althea for all her help."

"I will. Please know you're both always welcome."

They shook hands and then Sean took mine, kissing the back of it. "And thank you, Deborah, for your assistance with Eliza."

The short walk in the fresh morning air helped chase the thoughts of Sean and Eliza from my mind. Then it was filled with Catherine.

She met us in the hall. "There you are. It gave me such a fright to see Alvin rush in last night, worried over your well-being. Did you drink too much?"

"No, nothing like that, Aunt Catherine."

"She's still tired, Cathy. I'd like to get her to our room. We'll be down for the midday dinner," Alvin said as he gently steered me to the stairs.

"Shall I prepare tea?" she called after us.

"No!" I blurted, thinking of Uncle Jerald's warning.

"No, but thank you," Alvin said politely, hurrying me beyond the landing.

While I unpacked and saw to sorting the laundry for that week's pickup service, Alvin drew me a bath. The daytime soak was a luxury, but the marks on my middle were ghastly by sunlight.

Once I was wrapped in my dressing gown and the water swirled down the drain, we met in the sitting room. I fingered down his suspenders, smiling at the way he quickly took my hand so I wouldn't tickle him.

"Let's get you away from the front windows." He led me into the bedroom and sat on the edge of the bed, guiding me to stand before him. His hand rested on the knot of my sash. "How does it feel?"

"Much better, though it looks a fright."

He fingered the bow, and I nodded permission. He deftly untied the sash and opened my robe. His breath hitched as he took in the discoloring.

"Deb, you poor thing." He left a gentle kiss on my stomach. "I didn't know what to do with that ghostly vapor circling the room. When it slammed into you, I nearly died at the sight."

"The ectoplasm was more than I bargained for."

But Sean knew it was possible—and we were both aware of that.

Alvin pressed his lips together and retied my sash. As soon as we were cuddled on the bed, he whispered "I'm sorry you had to go through all that for me to believe you. I love you—I can now say—like I've loved no other."

"That's what matters most, Alvin."

His arms around me made me feel cherished, his kisses adored. We made love with the sunlight burning through the drapes as we fused another link of devotion between us.

The rest of the Sunday passed quietly. That night, I sealed our bedroom from unseen visitors before going to sleep—an event I expected to make habitual from then on.

Monday morning, I woke without troublesome dreams. I saw Alvin off for work then settled in the kitchen for a morning of baking. Once the chocolate cake was out of the oven, I went to the front porch for a few minutes of rest.

A woman, thin and precise, came up the front walk. Her hair was in a tight bun, her floral-print dress simple but pristine.

"Hello," I said as I stood from the rocking chair.

"Good morning. Might you be Deborah Farley?"

"I am. How may I help you?"

She stopped before me, no taller than my nose, yet her bearing demanded respect. "I'm Merritt Graves, a neighbor a few blocks down Palmetto. Sean asked me to stop by and introduce myself."

I drew back and she laughed.

"Yes, the old bounder begged me to make your acquaintance in an attempt to heal some rift I assume blossomed from one of his hair-brained schemes."

I nodded. "Would you like to sit down?"

I glanced in the front window to make sure Catherine wasn't in the parlor as we took adjacent rocking chairs.

"Well, Deborah—may I call you that?"

"Of course."

"And allow me to be Merritt to you. Sean came to me in tears yesterday afternoon, telling me he'd broken your trust and begging, as I already said, to help explain him to you since he's thoroughly disenchanted me before."

"Has he no shame?"

"None that he can't confess away," she said with a wry smile.

I grinned. "I completely understand."

"It was thirteen years ago he waltzed into my life. He hopped the fence at my aunt's house and nearly swept me away along with my younger cousin. I was your age and should have known better." She paused, gazing at me with understanding. "Sean said you saw him with my daughter the day you meet in Washington Square. We live across the street from the park."

Remembering the girl with glasses and a heavy soul, I nodded. "Ethelwynne, isn't it?"

"Yes. Ethelwynne and Andrew are my children. Sean has them both wrapped around his finger, but especially Winnie."

"Doesn't that worry you?"

"Some days more than others. His intelligence and charm are dangerous, dare I even save malevolent, to a degree. He was only seventeen when I met him, but practically my undoing." She sighed. "He's an arrogant cad, flashing that smile to be forgiven, and completely at a loss when he meets a woman that doesn't work with."

I laughed.

"I'm not sure what he did, but he's habitually hasty in his ideas and doesn't see beyond his nose when he's focused on something." She paused to study me. "Whatever line he crossed, know that he did so with pure intent. It's been years since I've witnessed such a level of moroseness in him. You're very special to him, Deborah. I won't tell you to forgive him or not, but understand he makes mistakes, though a lasting friendship with him is possible—if you want it."

"Thank you, Merritt. Would you like something to drink?"

"No, thank you. I need to get back to my laundry, but stop in on me anytime you feel like company. I'm home most days. If there's a dog in the yard, pay no mind. Velvet is a sweet girl. She just has a loud bark, especially if she has pups in the barn."

I accompanied Merritt to the sidewalk and hugged her in thanks before she went down the street, secure in my knowledge that Sean Spunner was even more of a rascal than I had initially thought.

Fifteen

Saturday morning was the football game. I cooked Alvin a breakfast twice the size as typical, complete with fresh-squeezed orange juice. Sean—whom I had avoided all week—was picking us up at half past eight so we could drive to the playing field. There, the blue team would practice for an hour before the red team arrived for a ten o'clock kickoff.

After cleaning the breakfast dishes, I found Alvin upstairs adjusting the pads in his gray football pants. He wore a long-sleeve, navy blue athletic shirt tucked into the belted wool pants and striped socks that went almost to his knees.

I put my arms around his middle and smiled up at him. "You look wonderful."

"And you'll be the most ravishing lady on the sidelines." He kissed me with a near ferocious passion.

Hands trailing his chest and shoulders, I returned the favor. "I like this rough, competitive side of you, Alvin."

He kissed across my neck and nuzzled my ear. "And I'll love you tonight, win or lose."

Alvin slung his cleats over his shoulder, and I piled my hair into a soft chignon topped with a navy bow that matched the trim on my walking suit.

After gathering the picnic basket filled with refreshments and jars of water, I was ready to go when Sean stopped in front of the house.

"Good morning, Farleys."

"Hello, Sean. Thanks for the ride," Alvin said as he handed me into the backseat.

I took the supplies from him and motioned Alvin to the front. The men immediately started a conversation about the forthcoming game.

"I'm putting you in charge of plays," Sean spoke as he drove. "Once you see how the men stand, you can assign them their positions too."

"That sounds like you're having Alvin do your job as team captain," I said.

Sean glanced over his shoulder at me, smirking. "Delegation is the best thing for a leader to do if he knows someone else would be better at something."

"Then delegate Alvin to team captain."

He laughed. "That's the one thing I can't do. Last year's teams vote on the captains, but I have no doubt Alvin will be a captain next time."

"You haven't even seen me play," Alvin said.

"No, but I had my secretary look up your stats from your years at Polytech. I have complete faith in you, *Dog* Farley. You're going to be the star player on the field today."

I already knew the nickname because my father was excited when he hired the former college football star the previous summer. Over supper one night, he explained to my mother that "Dog" didn't refer to him being ill-mannered or ugly (what she was concerned about), but to his full name—Alvin Robert Farley.

A.R.F.

I'd never do that to one of our children.

The game was to be held adjacent to Monroe Park, an entertainment area along Mobile Bay, south of the city. A wooden rollercoaster and baseball stadium rose above the tree line. A carousel, bandstand, arcade, and several eateries were sprinkled around the area, as well as many wandering souls displaced from hurricanes or those hanging onto pleasant memories from their earthly days.

I hugged Alvin's arm as Sean led us to the outskirts of the park. A grassy field was in the process of being marked by a couple of men with stakes to hammer into the ground to mark the yard lines along the sidelines. Alvin took a quick survey of the situation and steered me to a nearby magnolia tree. Underneath it, he spread our blanket, set the picnic basket on it, and removed his regular shoes to tie on his cleats.

Sean joined us with a handful of other men and introductions were made. Out of the ragtag group of pampered office men, Sean was the next-largest to Alvin. Not a good sign.

"Dog Farley!" One dark-haired man exclaimed. "I saw you play several times in oh-seven and eight against University of Alabama while I was a student. You were amazing!"

There were black slaps and jokes, then Sean urged them to the field.

The sky was an azure blue, the grass verdant green, and a cool breeze blew in from the bay. It was heavenly to experience such a scene even though a shadowy figure roamed the nearby seagrass as if looking for a lost child. I lay back on the blanket, listening to the shouts as the men tossed the ball and tried different offensive plays.

"Hey, Dog! Did you ever get hurt during a mass formation play while they were still legal?"

"Nothing to speak of, though I sent a couple guys to the hospital over the years."

Laughter followed, then Sean barked orders about lining up for a kick-off practice as a few latecomers walked over form the park.

"Miss Deborah," Chuck Brady called to me as he approached.

I sat up and smiled. "Hello, Mr. Brady."

"Call me Chuck. After that chess beating your husband gave me we're like kin now, right?"

I laughed. "Sure, Chuck. It's good to see you again."

He leaned closer. "Don't worry about being lonely. I've invited a bunch of girls to come watch the game. You'll have a gaggle of friends in no time."

"Brady!" Sean shouted. "Stop flirting with Dog's woman and get over here!"

"Dog?" Chuck looked from me to the team and back. "You mean to tell me Alvin is *the* Dog Farley?"

I nodded.

"We're gonna beat them reds today!" Chuck whooped a rebel yell and ran across the grass to join the others.

There wasn't a hesitant bone in Alvin's body has he taught plays and gave instructions the next half hour. I couldn't help smiling over his antics and the respect the others gave him.

Half a dozen men in red shirts arrived and huddled together near me as they looked at their competition.

"Who the hell is that?"

"Spunner said he recruited a new player."

"Look, he's got pads in his pants. Who does that?"

"Spunner, get your ass over here!" the guy who appeared to be in charge shouted.

"Watch your mouth, Thomas Charles. There's a lady right behind you. I don't think her husband would take too kindly to you talking like that in her vicinity."

The man glanced my way and his scowl turned surprised. "I beg your pardon, ma'am." He turned back to Sean. "If that's a collegiate player, I call a penalty."

"He's retired—two years out—and probably torn up from old injuries. He was a player when President Roosevelt threatened to ban the game. Do you think Dog Farley had anything to do with that?"

"Dog Farley? You must be shi—teasing us, Spunner," the red captain said with a sheepish look my way.

Sean crossed his arms and looked down his nose at the other man. "On my honor, Thomas Charles. And that's his wife right behind you. Mrs. Farley, meet our opponents, Thomas Charles and his band of red coats."

"Hello, gentlemen."

Dazed was the main expression, but a few nodded toward me.

"If you feel so encumbered by our teammate, we'll let you have the ball first without a coin toss."

"I don't need your charity, Spunner."

"Then we'll see you on the field in fifteen minutes. And by the way, this is our sideline."

The men in red shuffled away to await their other players and Sean advanced on me.

"Well, Deborah, how do I stand before you now?"

"Like an arrogant braggart, full of self-importance over another man's accomplishments."

A huge grin painted his face with smile lines while his whole body was surrounded in a blue tone that had nothing to do with his team. "I missed you this week. You're the only other woman besides Althea and Merritt who will call me out about my egotistical manners."

"Sending Merritt to me was rather sneaky."

"She likes you, Deborah. I hope you'll visit her sometime. She's alone too much during the day when the children are in school. Ah, here come some more neighbors." He nodded toward a group of young ladies. "Good morning, Miss Sadie. You and your friends are a bouquet of beauty this autumn day. Thank you for coming to cheer us on—no matter which team you're rooting for."

"We brought ribbons in both colors, so we can decide once we see the lineup," the blonde said.

"How very clever, though I'll put in a good word for the blue team." Sean winked. "This is our sideline. May I introduce our first fan of the day, Mrs. Deborah Farley. Deborah, this is Sadie Marley. She's just on the next block from us. Sadie, please introduce all the ladies to Deborah. I need to get back to the team."

"A new neighbor?" Sadie came forward as Sean retreated with a sly smile.

"My husband and I just moved from the Montgomery area the beginning of the month. It's nice to meet you, Sadie."

There was a flurry of introductions to the other five girls. Then all eyes were on the men though the others chattered between themselves.

"May we join you on the blanket?" Sadie asked.

"Only those for the blue team."

She laughed. "I suppose some of us will have to sacrifice the shade to go to the other side of the field."

A brunette scanned the players. "There's Henry! I have to go to the red side for him."

"Go on," Sadie told her. "I have to cheer for Sean since he's best friends with my sister's husband. My brother-in-law was supposed to be the doctor on site, but he got called in for an emergency surgery this morning."

"Who is that muscular man in blue?" someone asked. "He's bigger than Mr. Spunner."

All heads turned to where Alvin was leading the team in stretches. He might not belong to a fancy gym like the other men, but he kept in shape by lifting book stacks and stretching throughout the day.

"That's my Alvin. I didn't know him then, but he made a name for himself at Alabama Polytechnic Institute a few years back."

"How thrilling!" Sadie took my hand to look at my ring. "When were you married?"

"The day before we moved here. We're at the Snodgrass house on Rapier."

"With Catherine Snodgrass?" After I nodded, Sadie continued. "Mr. Snodgrass was kind, but—"

"You don't look much older than us," Another girl interrupted.

"I'm nineteen, and Alvin is twenty-five. He's a teacher at Barton Academy this year."

"Oh to be happily married at nineteen—that must be a dream come true."

Several groups of men, women, and families drifted over, some with folding chairs and others with blankets. By the time the team captains gathered in the center of the field with a man holding a coin, both sidelines boasted at least thirty viewers. The coin toss gave the ball to the blue team, to which Sean flashed a smirk at the other captain.

Thanks to Alvin's blocking, our team scored within the first two minutes. By the end of the first quarter, they were up by fifteen points and the crowd had tripled in size. Alvin guzzled water and was back on the field helping his team to another three touchdowns including one he ran across the goal line himself.

Alvin was swamped by his teammates in celebration of their twenty-five point lead at the end of the second quarter. He came for his refreshments, then wrapped me in a sweaty hug that took the breath from me.

"I'm a bit rusty, but it's going well," he said into my ear.

"You're marvelous, Alvin. Everyone I've heard says you're the best they've seen and it's the biggest crowd that's ever attended one of these games."

His smile grew even more. "It's a good group of guys."

"You should join the gym."

His brown eyes widened, and I nodded.

"Do it next week, Alvin. Monday, after school."

"Come on, Dog! You can love on your wife later. We've got a meeting to go to."

The players jostled each other away from the shade to a safe distance from their opponents.

As the game started in on its second half, Sadie pointed down the line of spectators. "See the man in a fedora with a notebook? That's Mr. Paterson, one of the main reporters for *The Mobile Register*. He doesn't typically cover sports, but I bet this game has a human interest angle with the crowd being so large."

My eyes wandered the expanse of people. I noticed the children who were with Sean the day I meet him—Merritt's Ethelwynne and Andrew. They were with a man who had to be their father, for they both favored him, right down to the wire-rimmed glasses Ethelwynne and the man both wore. All three were eagerly cheering, the youngest calling out Sean's name.

The remaining time passed in a blur of touchdowns and shouting. Sadie and I didn't talk continuously, but it was nice to know someone was with me in the sea of strangers. The end score: seventy-five to that lone red team touchdown. The players hoisted Alvin onto their shoulders and carried him across the field.

Sadie dropped her voice. "Does it scare you to be with him because he's so strong?"

"He's gentle and romantic when we're alone."

"He looks like he could be a barbarian."

"That might be interesting for a change."

We both giggled and then stepped out from under the tree to meet the team as they approached the sideline.

"Party at my house!" Sean announced. "Two o'clock until whenever everyone goes home!"

There were shouts and laughter from the team, then others moved in to congratulate the players.

Alvin kissed me long and deep. Whistles and catcalls surrounded us. I wanted to stay in his arms, but Alvin's attention was soon pulled to his teammates. Then the newspaper reporter made his way to the center of the crowd and wanted an interview. I migrated back to the blanket and settled in my old spot.

"It was wonderful meeting you," Sadie said, "but I need to catch the streetcar back to town. I hope to see you at Mr. Spunner's party."

As the crowd thinned, the noise level settled into a pleasant hum. I lay on my side, picking at the grass beyond the blanket's edge. A minute later, Sean approached.

"Allow me to help you pack while Alvin finishes his interview. Up you go, darling." Sean leaned close once I was on my feet. "I still dream about her most nights, but I can go hours during the day without thinking of Eliza. Thank you."

"It's nice not seeing her around you." I smiled. "I finished the Kardec book this week. I've decided I want to invoke Uncle Jerald, but I need you to help me sway Alvin to allow it."

A wicked glint came into his golden eyes. "It's the perfect day for that. High from the win, I'll see him properly liquored at the party, then you can have your way with him, Deborah."

***

Aunt Catherine and Tessa were both absent when we arrived home, so I prepared leftovers while Alvin showered. Not wanting to be interrupted if either returned, I carried the tray of food to our sitting room so we could dine in private. When I returned a second time with a pitcher of lemonade, Alvin was on the couch in his underdrawers. Slouched so his head could rest on the upholstered back, his legs were sprawled and his arms hung limp at his sides.

"Thirsty?"

"Parched," he answered.

I left the pitcher on his desk and brought him a glass.

"We're still alone," I said as he chugged the lemonade.

When it was empty, he set the glass on the side table and reached to where I stood. Once I was close enough, he grabbed my hips and settled me on one of his knees. His hand rubbed my back while the other trailed up my front until it wrapped my neck and drew me to his lips. We tasted and teased until we were almost breathless.

"Alvin," I said once I was curled against his chest and fingering his muscles. "Is this the old you, the new you, or the football you?"

"All of the above." His lips pressed my forehead with a lingering kiss. "That girl I thought I loved in college was eager to show her affection around game times. I'll admit I was cocky about it. Our displays got us in trouble a few times when we flaunted the school's regulations about appropriate behavior."

I kissed the base of his neck and hugged his warm torso.

"When she dropped me, I thought all ladies would spurn me because of my humble beginnings. I ignored the flirtations and denied my urges. It was easy until I met you." He lifted my chin so I would look into his eyes. "I fought my attraction to you for so long, I was shy and stilted even after it was safe to unbridle my feelings. Each week, I opened more to you, and when I thought I'd lost you last Saturday, the final restraints melted away. This is me, Deb. My heart is open and my body craves every connection it can get with you."

"I love all your complexities, Alvin."

"You're a fantasy, Deb—soft and strong and smart." He paused, gaze intent as he held me. "Do you think you're pregnant?"

"I have no idea. I think it would be too early to tell if I am. Why do you ask?"

"You were so delicate at the school when you came with my lunch, the nurse later asked me if you were with child. She said fainting was often a symptom, especially for first-time mothers." His hand caressed my stomach. "That's partly why I went to pieces when that vapor slammed into your middle last week. I feared for you and our possible child. I'm glad the bruising is almost gone."

"Alvin, my weakness that day was because of the sorrowful souls, but I look forward to bearing your children whenever that happens."

His eyebrows rose. "So we should keep trying?"

"Every day." The whispered words held all my longing. "I was made for you, Alvin."

Though not barbaric, Alvin was ardent and determined as we coupled. Wrapped in his arms, I clung to him and the feeling of euphoria he'd coaxed from me.

It was after three before we were presentable enough to leave the house, passing Tessa arriving for supper preparations. Alvin wore his navy college blazer and coordinating trousers, and I a simple shirtwaist and navy skirt. From across the street, the music and the hum of conversations and laughter rumbled.

Alvin didn't bother to knock, but walked right in the front door.

"Dog is here!" the shout went up.

The men in the hall were the first to clap him on the back, then more poured in from the parlor. It was a wave of white shirts—most with their sleeves rolled up—and not a pompadour to be seen.

"Deborah, I was hoping you'd come!" Sean took my hand and kissed it while Alvin was exchanging words with someone. "There's something I want to show you."

He led me through the smoke and clinking glasses to the far corner of the parlor. Hands on my waist, he hoisted me onto the lid of the grand piano.

"Sean!"

"I have a song for you, darling. I've been practicing all week."

"Hey, Dog! Spunner's got your wife on the piano like she's a trophy."

"She's the best prize I ever won," Alvin called back and raised a handled glass.

I waved to him as he watched from the doorway while sipping his foamy beer.

Sean sat on the piano bench and started on a jazzy tune. The words began with his peppy voice that quieted the room.

"'Two sweethearts courted happily for quite a while, the simple life of country folk…'" He went through the chorus and both verses of "Some of These Days" and I heard the message between the lyrics.

Please don't give up on me. I need you in my life, and will be there for you and Alvin in return.

At the end of the song, I jumped down and kissed his cheek. "Thank you, Sean."

Grinning, he tucked my arm around his. "What would you like to drink?"

"Could I try a beer?"

"Heavens no—it's horrible. Only the men who were short on cash at college got hooked on that. You're much better off with something aged or a mixed drink. We need to get Alvin adjusted to the finer things in life. That should be easy since he has you." Sean leaned in conspiratorially. "That's why you were late, isn't it? He had you as a celebratory—"

I punched his arm with my free hand and the audience of watchful men responded with whistles and shouts.

"Spunner's getting fresh with the lady!"

"Sean Spunner is as annoying as one of my brothers," I declared and crossed the room to Alvin.

Beaming with the attention, Alvin slung an arm around my waist and kissed me. If the sour taste was an indication of the beer, then Sean was right about beverage choices. Alvin's hands splayed over my backside. Hungry and demanding, we kissed with freed passion to the sounds of a rowdy audience. Apparently, an act of Congress and God were equal to a horde of football players when it came to Alvin relaxing his standards, and I relished every moment.

Before he had a chance to release me, a knock sounded on the front door.

Someone behind us opened it, then a whistle silenced those nearest the hall.

"Why Miss Marley, what can we do for you?"

"I'm looking for Deborah. Does this work as my entrance pass?" Sadie waved her blue ribbon at the man at the door, her other hand on the hip of her polka dot dress.

I met her at the door, smiling at the brazenness of the young woman.

"Deborah!" Sadie came for a hug. Glancing about the noisy space, she leaned to my ear. "Are we the only ladies?"

"Yes, so far. I was just about to get a drink. Let's find our host."

Sean had retreated to the library, huddled around the decanters with several other men. When he saw us, his eyes widened.

"Miss Sadie, what are you up to, darling?"

"What type of welcome is that, Mr. Spunner?"

"An honest one." He kissed her cheek in welcome.

"I'm here to keep Deborah company."

"Is that so?"

She nodded, eyes straying around the room.

"We're looking for a drink," I said. "Give us something worthy, please."

He nodded and motioned to the chaise. "Make yourselves comfortable, ladies."

As soon as we were seated, Chuck joined us.

"Miss Sadie, it's good to see you."

"Hello, Mr. Brady." She smiled. "It was an excellent game today."

"Might I collect a kiss for assisting in the win?"

Sadie crooked her finger at him and he leaned over.

"No, Deborah first," Sadie said.

He looked at me with wide eyes, but I quickly kissed his cheek.

Grinning, Chuck turned his other cheek to Sadie. At the last second, she changed her approach. Her lips met his, and he nearly feel into her lap at his surprise.

Sean, arriving with our drinks, laughed while Chuck collected a good ribbing from his friends.

Sadie accepted her glass. "This isn't champagne or wine."

"No, ma'am." Sean crossed his arms.

Sadie slung it back in one swallow. I took a tentative sip, then coughed.

"Drink it fast," she urged me.

"No, darlings, slow and easy is better," Sean said. "Enjoy the flavor of the bourbon, but don't go too long without eating. There's a spread of food in the dining room."

When he swaggered away, I caught Alvin smiling at me from the chess board. He was seated across from the red team captain.

"Let's go look around," Sadie said. "Don't stand too close, though. I want to be approachable."

We roamed the corridor, nibbled some shrimp and cheese in the dining room, then entered the parlor.

Seeing a quiet corner, I led Sadie to it. "Are you a believer?"

Sadie laughed. "A believer? I go to Mass every week."

"You believe in God—a higher power—and spirits and everything?"

"Yes, as much as the next person. But what I find the most thrilling is spiritualism."

I took both of her hands in mine. "Could you come to our house at eleven tonight? I'm going to attempt to invoke Alvin's uncle, Jerald Snodgrass."

Her lips curled into a grin. "To ask him if his wife killed him? My mother always thought she might have because—all the neighbors knew it—she often had men callers while he was at work."

"What?"

Sadie nodded. "I tried to tell you before the game when you told me where you lived. My mother hates Mrs. Snodgrass, and she's the kindest lady alive. My mother invites every lady in the neighborhood to tea at least once a year—all except Catherine Snodgrass. She came one time the year she moved in but never since."

"I wasn't planning on asking anything of that sort, but of family matters pertaining to Alvin. There might be somethings that are better not shared, so discretion—"

"I know how to keep secrets, Deborah. Is Chuck coming?" Her eyes roamed the space until she caught his gaze.

"I'd like to keep things simple and intimate, so just you and Sean."

"Will I get to hold the old man's hand?" She giggled.

"It's a serious business, Sadie. We need to be united and sober and—"

"Then we better keep Sean away from the whiskey."

Chuck wandered over and took Sadie's hand. "Will you sit with me?"

She nodded and he claimed the corner with an oversized chair, just big enough for the two of them. His wavy dark hair was several inches above her blonde crown as they whispered back and forth. Then their lips met, lingering more than the quick one offered before.

"She's a brazen one, but her big sister was like that too before she married," Sean said. "I can't image you casually kissing on someone like that."

"I never did."

The voices in the house rose and fell with the different conversations and antics, but beyond the din was a calmness I had never experience around Sean. No lost loves hanging nearby. No Eliza tormenting me with her bawdy humor. Enjoying the peace, I wandered to the kitchen.

After a hug, Althea handed me a tray loaded with fresh fruit cups and cold shrimp, and pointed to the door. "Sean Francis catered the food, Deborah, so I'm not overworked. Get out there and have fun. I'll see you another day."

I carried the tray to the dining room, then settled in the parlor. Despite the antics around me, I found an inner focus on Uncle Jerald and my plans to commune with him. Aunt Catherine typically went upstairs before ten. Alvin, Sean, and Sadie would be my united circle for concentration. I was certain it would work. Alvin's strength would protect us from physical dangers, and I would protect us from spiritual perils, should they arise. Jerald Snodgrass was, after all, less difficult than Eliza Melling.

Sixteen

Half an hour later, Alvin perched on the arm of my chair.

"I think Sean is trying to get me drunk. I've had four beers and three shots, but he keeps pushing me to take more whiskey. These men might be used to that, but I'm not."

"I know what you need." I stood, kissing his cheek before leading the way through the crowded hall to reach the front door.

"Where ya goin', Dog?" Chuck asked.

"Out for a walk," I replied in Alvin's behalf. "We'll be back before long."

In the cooler air, Alvin took a deep breath. "Yes, this is helpful, Deb. Thank you."

I smiled and headed east on Palmetto, rounding the corner at Chatham to the gate in the wrought iron fence.

"Sean's friends live here. I met Merritt this week, and her husband and children watched the game this morning. I'm sure they'd love to meet you."

When we passed through the gate, a dog barked and ran for us.

"Velvet!" Merritt called from the side of the house.

The dog woofed once in reply.

"Who's there?" she called.

"It's Deborah," I said as she came around the left side of the house. "And Alvin Farley."

"Deborah, it's good to see you. And Mr. Farley. I heard about you this past hour." She smiled and increased her pace, then motioned to her dog. "This is Velvet. Velvet, Deborah and Alvin are friends. Offer your hand."

The dog sat and lifted a paw for us to shake.

I laughed as I shook it, and then stroked the dog's neck. "She's beautiful and soft, not to mention well-trained."

Merritt laughed. "Velvet is the best sales girl. If you ever decide you want a puppy, let me know. I raise one or two litters a year, but they go quickly. Would you like to come in for some iced tea?"

"Thank you. That does sound nice."

We followed her around the side of the house she'd appeared from. There was a mass of bed linens hanging on the clotheslines and beyond that a small grove of citrus trees sparkling with colorful bottles hanging from the branches. I felt like I was in the country though we were in the middle of a city neighborhood.

"Oranges?" I asked.

"Satsumas, which are just as good. I'm happy to share when they ripen, especially when friends help pick them."

"We'd be glad to assist," Alvin said as Merritt's son ran towards us from across the yard with a mitt and baseball in his hand.

"Are you Dog Farley?" the boy asked.

Alvin smiled. "Last time I checked. What's your name?"

"Drew Graves. I prefer baseball, but you were terrific in the game today."

"I played some ball when I was growing up. Show me what you've got."

The boy backed up and threw the ball to Alvin.

"That will keep them busy a while, and I'm sure Bart will hear and join them before long. He's working on a project in the stable with Ethelwynne. Let's go inside." Merritt held the screen door open. Velvet and I followed her through the utility porch and into a cheery blue and white kitchen. I sat at the square table.

Through the open hall door, a hazy figure entered.

"We have breakfast here each morning," Merritt said as she poured the tea without so much as a glance at the spirit. "And dinner—whoever is home with me. I save the formality of the dining room for supper."

"That's a lovely idea." I tried to keep my voice even as the shadow moved closer. "I tend to perch on a stool in the kitchen if I eat alone."

Merritt brought our glasses over and sat across from me. "How is Sean behaving himself?"

The spirit shimmered in a burst of clarity, showcasing a dark-haired young woman, cherubic face bright with innocence.

"Very well the past few days, though I kept away from him last week."

"That's understandable. I'm glad you came this afternoon, Deborah. Bartholomew and the children said that your husband was the best football player they've ever seen. Andrew was hoping to be introduced, but there were reporters and so many others around the team, Bart insisted they go home rather than wait around."

We appreciate your thoughtfulness in sharing your time.

I stared at the girl, still shining in her human form like an opal in the sun, and marveled at the appearance of two more beings beside her—parents, perhaps, but she didn't favor either of them with their sharp features.

Take her hand, the older woman told me. *Tell her these words.*

I reached across the table to Merritt, taking her slim hand in mine. "You're not alone, Merritt. Your departed family members watch over you and your children."

She gasped and looked about, but I kept her hand.

"Winifred is beautiful. I can see why Sean was captivated by her radiance. And the couple is proud of how you're keeping the house and Bartholomew the store. They all love you and your family."

When I finished the message, I tried to withdraw my hand, but Merritt clung to it, tears streaming down her face. "I'm always melancholy this time of year. Yellow fever took Uncle Andrew in September and Winnie that October thirteen years ago. Sean didn't set you up to this, did he?"

I laughed. "No, and I'm sorry to have sprung that on you, but they wanted you to know. I wasn't expecting to see them when I came. I did see a glimpse of Winifred that first day I met Sean. She and Eliza were following him around."

Merritt released my hand and retrieved a handkerchief. As she dabbed her cheeks an exasperated laugh escaped. "Eliza was the worst thing that ever happened to Sean in the time that I've known him." She studied my face several moments. "I suppose you have a second sight like he does, but different."

I nodded, awed that once more, someone accepted all I said without question.

We stayed inside until we finished our drinks. Once in the yard, I was introduced to Bartholomew and Ethelwynne.

It was more than a quarter of an hour later when Alvin insisted we return to Sean's party. On our walk back, I told him of seeing Merritt's deceased family members.

"Their message was of love and peace." I squeezed his hand as we strolled down the sidewalk. "That brings to mind my idea of contacting Uncle Jerald to help set you at ease about the inheritance. May I have your permission to invoke him, Alvin?"

"Well, I…"

"If he doesn't wish to come or speak—that's up to him."

"But you were forceful with Eliza's ghost."

"That was a completely different situation, Alvin. She was already here and causing trouble. Invocation isn't like that. It's politely asking the spirit if they would like to communicate and letting them know you are ready to listen."

He sighed and ran his free hand over his jaw. "I suppose you could try, Deb."

***

Alvin and I stayed at the party two more hours. When we said goodbye, Sean promised to run off the remainder of his guests at ten, then collect Sadie so they could arrive at our house together, creating the least possible disturbance to the household.

"I had Tessa save supper for you," Catherine said as soon as we were in the house. "The food is in the icebox."

"Thank you, Cathy," Alvin said. "We've had plenty to eat for now. Sean hosted a terrific party after our win."

"So the game went well? No injuries?"

"All is well for me, but I can't say the same for the other team." Alvin grinned.

I kissed him and whispered, "I'll see you upstairs."

I left without bidding goodnight to Catherine. Not wanting anything to disturb my peace as I prepared for the invocation, I figured limiting my interaction with the woman was best.

After stripping to my underclothes, I washed my face before turning for the bedroom. Alvin had his jacket and shirt off and was ready to open his trouser fasteners.

"Don't get too comfortable," I warned him. "We have visitors coming at eleven."

"What?"

"Sean and Sadie. They're going to help us with my invocation."

Alvin took me by the shoulders. "That sounds an awful lot like a séance."

Looking up at his earnest gaze, I gave him a soft smile as my arms snaked around his middle. "I suppose that's one way to label it."

"Deb—"

I stopped him with a kiss that he fortunately took full advantage of. Rather than letting him lead as I had that afternoon, I guided his movements to escalate the urge. Release would help clear my head and relax him as well. That was my end goal, but I enjoyed every delightful moment leading up to it.

A pounding on the door started right after Alvin's pinnacle.

"You two sound like animals in heat!" Catherine called before stomping away and slamming her door.

Looking down at Alvin's flushed face, I grinned. "Dog Farley bought passion to the bedroom tonight."

He moved to lift me, but I clung to my position.

"Deb, we sh—"

"Alvin Robert Farley, this is *your* house and we're married. There's nothing to feel shame over. What we just shared was wonderful—a beautiful, unrestrained coupling that binds us together like nothing else can. Don't let her take that away." I trailed my hands over his bare chest. "I've waited weeks to see you unleash the ardor you have today."

"It has felt good." He gave a shy grin. "The best ever."

"Please don't take this from me, Alvin."

He gently rolled us to our sides and kissed me with tender care. "I'll never give you up, Deborah."

He held me as we kissed, but I saw the tiredness sweep him, body and soul, with the fading of his aura from its typical bright red.

"Rest, Alvin." I left a kiss on his soft lips. "I'll wake you before the others arrive."

He nodded, a slight upward curve to his mouth as his hand trailed my middle while I shifted to sit up. "Do you think having a bit of me in you will help you connect with my uncle when you call to him?"

A different man might have said that as a joke, but Alvin was sincere.

"I'm not sure, but it won't hurt my cause, at any rate." I leaned over to kiss him once more, pleased that he had accepted this part of me and was trying to understand it. "Thank you for helping."

He took my hand before I could straighten. "I love you, Deb. Don't let Sean talk you into anything asinine."

"There's no chance of that. I'm in control tonight."

His grin let me know he'd enjoyed my show of dominance in bed, but that wasn't where my leading would end.

I quietly washed and dressed, choosing a lacy purple tea gown I'd been given on my seventeenth birthday, and pulling my hair into a loose pompadour.

The sitting room was lit only by Alvin's green-shaded desk lamp. Enjoying the earthy glow, I knelt beside the little couch in quiet pondering. It wasn't so much a prayer as it was a call to center myself on the present. I wrestled with my thoughts of Alvin—our shared desires—and cleared the memory of the football game. I did send a plea to God to remind Sean of his promise to arrive barefoot and calm with Sadie, armed with studious and reflective on thoughts of Jerald Snodgrass, whom both had met a few times in passing. That tiny connection was better than none.

At a quarter to eleven, I woke Alvin with a caress on his bare arm. "It's time."

He nodded and stretched.

"Don't bother to put shoes on. I'll be downstairs."

Catherine had made no sound nor left her bedroom since her outburst nearly two hours previous, but I went barefoot down the stairs as quietly as possible. I paused on the landing by the stained glass window, the geometric design eerie with only the quarter moon to light it. I shivered and took the final few steps to the left into the kitchen. I unlocked the backdoor so it would be open to the screened porch, allowing Sean and Sadie to let themselves in when they arrived.

From the hutch in the dining room, I retrieved silver candlesticks. Creating a circle of five, I lit the tapers and turned off the electric lights. The yellow glow flickered in the warm air currents.

"Deb?" Alvin said in a soft voice from the parlor at the same time Sean and Sadie silently entered from the back hall.

"Thank you," I said to them, motioning to their bare feet. Turning to Alvin, I saw the Kardec book in his hand and concern on his face. "Yes?"

He opened the book and pointed. "It says right on the first page that this guide is for 'the difficulties and the dangers that are to be encountered in the practice of spiritism.' You've been hurt before. I don't want to see you in pain again, Deb."

I stepped to Alvin and took the book from him, the lace on my skirt brushing his trousers cuffs. "I've finished reading it and have more experiences to draw upon. You knew your uncle in life. Was he a kind man?"

"Yes, but—"

"He'll be of the same temperament in death, Alvin. If he comes, we have nothing to fear from him. Believe in my abilities which you've already seen in action."

He nodded and our lips met. Alvin's arms went around me and then Sean took the book. I embraced Alvin in return and continued the kiss.

"Come on, Farleys," Sean said a few moments later. "Don't you need to focus, Deborah?"

"Alvin helps ground me," I replied.

Sadie's giggling caused Alvin to straighten.

"Excuse our display, Miss Sadie." His hand nervously adjusted his navy suspenders.

"It was marvelous," she said in reply, to which Alvin blushed.

Sean placed the book on the table, took Sadie's elbow, and joined us within the entranceway of the pocket doors that separated the dining room and parlor. "Tell us what you need, Deborah."

"We all need to prepare our thoughts, focusing on Jerald Snodgrass with the desire for good and a faith that he will manifest himself."

Sadie nodded. The lavender glow about her pulsed with excitement. "But what is it you wish to ask him?"

"Why he changed his will," I said, planning to keep as much information private as possible.

"He made me the main beneficiary this past winter without informing Cathy," Alvin told the others. "She was livid when the will was read after his funeral."

"Who was his solicitor?" Sean asked.

"Mr. Joyce. I went back to him during my first week here to sign papers naming Deborah my sole beneficiary."

"He's a solid chap, but you know I'd give you both more attention and care if you wish to move your business to Finnigan and Spunner."

Sadie practically snorted a laugh. "You're a bore, Sean. We're here for spiritualism and you speak of business. Deborah said we need to focus."

"This is about a will, and that *is* part of my business dealings, darling."

She rolled her eyes.

"All of us have to be in accord—no ill feelings are allowed." I looked between Sadie and Sean.

"I adore, Sean," she said with a smile while linking her arm around his. "He's entertaining on the football field, hosted a wonderful party, and knows the handsomest men in town. There's nothing not to like about the old bachelor, though I enjoy teasing him."

He inclined his head and offered a smug grin. "And I'll never have ill feelings toward a pretty woman."

"Then we'll proceed." I took Alvin's right hand in my left, and Sean's left in my right. Without instruction, Sadie captured their free hands from her position across from me. "Think of Jerald Snodgrass, any positive memories you have of him, or just his image. No one speak once I verbally invoke his name. Is that clear?"

They all nodded.

"If he appears, do not try to touch him or speak to him. I will communicate for us." With a nod, I shifted my feet slightly apart. "Let us begin. Start by feeling your feet grounding you to this world even as your mind is reaching for heaven. Allow the strength of the house, the firmament of the very floors Jerald Snodgrass walked upon, to hold you to this special location. Now close your eyes and feel those tethers, opposite but equal."

I squeezed Alvin's firm hand, then Sean's, which was damp with perspiration. No matter his eagerness to experience things, he was nervous.

"Focus on the connection between us. We are linked in purpose, thinking of Jerald, and asking, in the name of God the Father, if Jerald Alvin Snodgrass will communicate with us this night."

Pausing to allow time to reflect and seek a response, the silence wrapped around me like a scarf wound too tightly, as though the house was holding its breath and trapping me in it.

"We only wish to speak to Jerald Snodgrass, the former occupant of this home," I said with what I hoped was enough authority. Alvin squeezed my hand. "No other spirits are to speak. No one else may disturb the peace within these walls."

I opened my eyes and found Sadie staring at me with fear. I offered a smile and shook my head, hoping she understood I meant nothing else was there—yet. Her eyes darted about the space before she closed them.

"Uncle Jerald Snodgrass, Alvin wishes to know something that only you can tell him. Will you come to us in the light that we might ask?"

The candles flickered, but I saw nothing.

Alvin's thumb caressed the side of my hand, as though communicating he was okay with it not working.

"If you can come, Uncle Jerald, Alvin would appreciate it. He's been concerned about you placing him over your wife, not fully utilizing the house or money as his own."

The flames flickered. One candle went out as a cold breeze stirred between the rooms. A shadow the size of a screech owl loomed next to the dining table. It grew into the size and shape of a heavier-set version of Alvin.

"Hello, Uncle Jerald," I said to the opaque figure now hovering behind Sean and Sadie.

Seeing where my eyes looked, Sadie squeaked and flinched, but Sean and Alvin held her hands firmly. Alvin, unblinking, watched as the ghost of his uncle passed through the linked hands of our friends and entered the circle we'd made.

You look well, Alvin. Jerald's voice sounded raspy in my mind. *What do you wish to know?*

I looked at the others. "Can you see him?"

They all nodded.

"Can you hear him?"

Alvin shook his head, his brow furrowed. Sean shrugged and looked discouraged, and Sadie frowned.

"Not everyone in this world is ready to communicate with your side, Uncle Jerald," I explained. "Alvin has given me permission to speak in his behalf."

Alvin looked from his uncle's spirit to me and back, nodding.

"Alvin wants to understand why you blessed him with such abundance."

I built this house for Cathy, but she defiled it. I wanted neither my home nor money in the hands of an adulterous woman.

"Oh…" Not sure how to respond, I watched the ghost turn towards the far doorway of the dining room.

Since his attentions were still elsewhere, I spoke to the others. "He knew Catherine was an adulterer."

Jerald nodded, and turned back to me. *I left her enough to live on without worry, though she will have to watch her spending to make it last.* He paused. *She is in the kitchen.*

"Excuse me." I released the men but I still felt Uncle Jerald's presence.

I rushed to the kitchen and found Catherine fiddling with something in the icebox.

"Who's the kitchen pirate now?" I demanded as I crossed the tile floor.

Catherine jumped, a guilty look soon turning to anger as she straightened her silk dressing gown. "I was only curious if Alvin had eaten the leftovers yet."

Her pocket, Jerald's words came to me.

There was a definite bulge in the hip pocket of her robe.

Poison.

Anger flashed and I advanced. "If you have any ideas about harming Alvin, you'll meet vengeance!"

"You're a silly child." She shut the door of the icebox with enough force to rattle the bottles inside.

"Did you kill your husband?" A cold breeze whipped through the room with my words.

"How dare you accuse me?" she whispered with a vileness I could feel in the charged air. "He had a weak heart and died in his sleep. I loved Jerald—I did! I stayed by his side though his health was no longer prime. I loved him until that afternoon in the lawyer's office when I realized he didn't love me. He cared for his nephew more because he might carry on the family tree when I couldn't."

A cabinet opened slightly, then slammed shut.

Alvin had mentioned his uncle was disappointed in not having children. "Then why were you having an affair?"

Catherine laughed. "You can't blame me for amusing myself when my husband requested so little. I'm still in fine form and was planning on cozying up with Alvin when he moved here. You had to ruin that with your speedy wedding. He had never breathed a word about a girl up north. You must have trapped him into it."

My face heated because, until recently, I thought I'd done exactly that.

"What, did I strike a sour cord, little miss?" She laughed. "Alvin could have done much better than you, with or without money."

"No I couldn't have. Nor do I ever want a woman other than Deborah." Alvin entered the kitchen with the words.

"She's nothing but a child, Alvin Farley. You'd be better off with me, but it's too late for that."

"She has poison in her pocket," I whispered as I took his hand.

Catherine laughed. "What, my bottle of laudanum? I keep it in my dressing gown pocket so I can access it on my sleepless nights. It's a prescription I've needed since Jerald died." Catherine allowed her chest to heave in a prelude to manufactured sobs.

"She was going to poison the leftovers, if she hasn't already. Uncle Jerald warned me."

"The imaginings of this girl are simply ridiculous." Catherine approached, a hand going to Alvin's forearm. "I don't see how you tolerate her."

He lifted her hand off his arm with a snarled lip. "I don't see how we've tolerated *you* this long. You need to leave, Cathy. Tonight."

A rush of cold air swirled through the room. I knew Sean and Sadie were just around the corner, but Uncle Jerald was with us. His form shimmered behind Catherine.

I had my suspicions, but when the cook told me after Cathy had left the supper table my final night that she'd had a man upstairs all afternoon, I knew. I died in the bed she shared with him, smothered by her perfumed pillow.

"You fired the old cook!" I blurted. "She told Jerald that you'd had a man over and you got rid of her, probably because she suspected you of doing away with him."

"The doctor said he died in in sleep from heart failure. He went peacefully. You can't prove anything."

I advanced without Alvin, but Uncle Jerald was beside me. "You smothered him with your pillow!"

Face white with fear, Catherine's arms raised to strike. Alvin pulled me back and Sean and Sadie entered the kitchen from the hall.

"I've telephoned the police, Alvin," Sean said, eyes sweeping the room until they fell on Jerald's ghost.

"None of you can prove anything!" Catherine screeched.

Jerald floated toward his wife, his form solidifying. Catherine paled as the temperature dropped, causing me to shiver. His figure continued to brighten until it exploded into a million particles like the burst of a firework, causing everyone to flinch.

The shimmering pieces swirled and regrouped into a pulsating mass of demonic green flames that lapped our feet like a scourge. Sadie clung to Sean, and Alvin placed himself between it and me.

"You're a murderer, Catherine, and everyone here knows it," I said around Alvin's shoulder.

Catherine looked from Sean to Alvin, then to Sadie's wide eyes, feeling the weight of their judgmental stares as her guilty eyes darted between the witnesses. With a cry of frustration, she dashed for the back stairs.

Slowly, the green smoke faded.

Sadie looked flushed. Sean brought her to the sofa, Alvin and I silently following.

"I don't think I'm up for this spiritualism thing after all," Sadie whispered and then fainted, slumping against the back of the sofa.

Sean sighed, then chuckled. "Not all girls are as tough as Deborah."

"Deb could endure everything when I wanted to hide from the truth," Alvin said.

I put my arms around him. "We're one in purpose now."

"Yes," he agreed with a smile. "United with my miraculous wife in our own home. Uncle Jerald's inheritance is a blessing, but I'm sorry he passed the way he did."

When Sadie woke from her stupor, Sean pulled a flask out of his jacket pocket. They both took a few nips while Alvin was poised near the hall, listening for movement from Catherine upstairs.

"How long until the police come, Sean?" I asked.

"What? Oh, I was bluffing to see if she would admit anything. Obviously she's guilty. Jerald Snodgrass says she killed him, and if I were you, I'd toss everything out of the icebox, just to be safe."

"I will, but you should really telephone them now."

"I will, darling." He stood and kissed my cheek. "You were marvelous."

Sean went to the back hall where the telephone box was near the kitchen.

A moment later, scuffling came from upstairs. The *clap-click* of heeled shoes down the wood hall. Catherine's satin shoes were the first thing visible between the carved banister slats. Then her long skirt and suitcase. And a gleam of something more.

I'm not sure which happened first—the suitcase dropping or the entanglement of her quickening feet—but she went down. Head over heels, she flipped the final six steps. She tumbled across the little landing and straight through the stained glass window.

Sadie shrieked, but Alvin lunged for the stairs, staring out the shattered window at the scene below.

"What the hell was that?" Sean ran in.

We joined Alvin on the landing, looking down at Catherine's twisted body impaled on the picket fence between the neighbor's house and ours.

"I hate to say it," Sean said, "but that's the best justice. The courts couldn't have seen it through as efficiently."

"Come on, Deb. You don't need to see that." Alvin tucked me to his side and led me back to the parlor.

As my role with Uncle Jerald was officially complete, I allowed the men to deal with the police when they arrived. My new concern was comforting the frantic Sadie.

Epilogue

On the morning of November first, I had just slid a loaf of sourdough bread into the oven when the back screen door snapped shut, setting the yellow curtains fluttering.

Sean strode in—his habit several times a week of late since he knew I could be found in the kitchen any given morning.

"You look awful." I wiped my hands on my apron. "I'm glad Alvin and I didn't go to the Halloween Flirts dance if a hangover was part of the deal. Sadie didn't warn me of that."

Sean grinned and rubbed a hand over his unshaved jaw. "I didn't stay long and drank three times as much at home as I did at the dance. I was the oldest guest, which Sadie teased me about. You and Alvin would have been the only married couple, but that wouldn't have stopped the girls from flocking to him. They're downright vicious when in costume."

I laughed. "It couldn't be that bad."

"Just wait until you see a Mardi Gras masquerade. Besides, I did nothing but think of Eliza there."

"Why is that? You've been doing good lately."

"They used many of the old props she'd painted for the group five years ago. The Halloween Flirts dance was the night we first—"

I snapped a towel at him. "Never mind. I remember."

"But I'm done with her, Deborah, and she's gone for good." He hopped onto the counter by the sink and crossed his arms. "Don't you want to know how and why?"

"Let me fix some coffee, and we'll sit at the table like civilized people."

I set out a plate with the remainder of yesterday's cornbread along with a dish of honey butter. Sean smiled his thanks as he slathered a chunk.

After a few sips of coffee, he sighed and leaned back in his chair. "I looked straight at her painting and said 'I promised I'd never forget you when we were parted. I've kept my end of the bargain nearly five years. Is it enough?' In response, she shook her head and stepped out of the painting."

My cup clattered to the table. "You saw her?"

"In all her natural glory!" He bit his lip. "She chased me around the house, taunting me. And then she confessed."

"Confessed?"

"That she was unfaithful to me."

Tears welled in the corner of his eyes, and I remembered my words when I banished Eliza into the painting.

"I'm sorry, Sean."

"But you knew." His keen mind never missed anything. "You bound her there until she unburdened herself."

I patted his hand and straightened in my chair. "Yes. And she felt guilty for her actions. That's why she was being faithful to you by following you around."

"A tigress hunting me." His dimples flashed with a smile. "But hearing that cleared the last of my feelings for her. I burned her sketches in the fireplace."

"You did not!"

"I did. And I nearly tossed the painting too, but she talked me out of it. It's gone, though. I tucked it in the closet like Dorian Gray trying to hide his indiscretions. The folly of my youth."

"You were twenty-five—the same as Alvin. Did he make a mistake marrying me?"

"Don't fish for compliments, darling." He took another bite before continuing. "Eliza told me to wait a few more years, then find a woman better than her and Winifred combined."

"And that was it?"

Sean nodded. "She stepped back into the painting and everything has been quiet. Do you want to come over and see for yourself?"

"I will after supper, then you and Alvin can have a game of chess. Finish your coffee and I'll see you this evening."

Sabine arrived while Sean was still at the table. She blushed and avoided eye-contact with him.

"Thanks for the coffee and food, Deborah. I feel human now. Warn Alvin I'll be sober by the time we have our chess match tonight." Sean stood, kissed the back of my hand, and winked at Sabine on his way out.

Tessa didn't return after Catherine died, but I hoped she was able to go back to her old job. Sabine was happy to be reduced to two partial days a week, allowing her the opportunity to work at other houses and earn more money. She came for several hours Tuesday and Friday mornings, helping me with deep cleaning because Alvin refused to think of me scrubbing floors. Sabine also helped me arrange the new furnishings Alvin and I had purchased. We'd kept the front rooms upstairs, but the large back room was empty—for now.

After my midday meal, I went across town for an appointment and stopped at Barton Academy on my way home. The final bell had just rung. I waited outside the gate for the bulk of the students to file out before making my way to the third floor. A habited nurse floated by in the stairwell, and a few moans were heard through the walls, but I wasn't oppressed by the sensations.

I stopped in Alvin's open classroom door, watching him at the chalkboard with two students as he solved an equation and explained his reasoning.

"Thank you, Mr. Farley," one said.

The other student nodded. "It makes sense now."

"I expect all your answers to be correct tomorrow." Alvin wiped his chalky hands on a handkerchief. "Have a good afternoon, boys."

The students bid me good day as they hurried out.

Alvin looked over and grinned. "Deb, what a surprise."

"I finished my errands and thought we could walk home together."

"You never told me what appointment you had."

"It was with Dr. Hughes." I took his hand. "Alvin, we're going to be parents."

His brown eyes widened before the smile found his lips. "You're sure? Truly sure? Has it been long enough?"

"Yes on all accounts. June is the estimated timing."

He hugged me to his chest. "Then I'll have plenty of time with you and the baby over next summer. Deb, it's perfect. Thank you for telling me now rather than waiting until I got home."

After a glance at the door to be sure we weren't seen, Alvin's hot lips pressed to mine in a way that sent me spiraling into paradise. My hands trailed his shoulders and around his neck, clinging to his strength and unbridled passion.

When the kiss ended, Alvin didn't let me go. "I look forward to watching you grow into motherhood."

Hugging him back, I smiled in return. "There's no one I'd rather be on that journey with than you."

THE END

Author's Note

Since the cover is often the first thing noticed about a book, I'll start things off with a huge THANK YOU to Amanda Herman. This is the fourth book she's done an original watercolor for. Once again, she captured my vision while staying true to her own tone. I love the subtle Gothic whimsy she captured for the Farleys.

Melissa Miller welcomed me into her home and gave me a tour so I could better visualize the main setting of this book. I'm sure Alvin and Deborah Farley would have been as comfortable in the house with their family as you've been with yours.

Alisha Vincent was a huge help in recommending a documentary to me about mediumship. And Jeff D. Johnston pointed me in the right direction for all things historic football, allowing me to set the stage for that game at Monroe Park, complete with proper scoring numbers.

A thunderous "War Eagle" to Janet Gignillait and Amber Guy for guiding me in the right direction during my search for information about Alabama Polytechnic Institute football in the early 1900s. Their input brought me to John C. Varner with Auburn University Libraries Special Collections & Archives and Clint Richardson with Auburn Uniform Database, who answered my email questions. Thank you, gentlemen. Sometimes no documentation is insightful in itself.

A giant thank you to beta reader Jennifer Lamont and critique partner Candice Marley Conner for all their input. And my appreciation to Carmel Allen and Stephanie Graham, members of Dalby's Darklings, for choosing names for the girls' math teacher and the nurse at Barton Academy.

Special appreciation goes to Sean Connell for once again nudging me—okay, sometimes more than nudging me (there were all caps involved this time)—back onto the right track after I've been led astray by mischievous characters. The finished product is much stronger than anything I can do alone. I'll continue to hold the banana bread.

In closing, my gratitude forever goes to my family for their continued support. I know I'm not the easiest person to live with when characters are trying to take over all my thinking, but it does keep me sane in the long run. Thank you all, especially John for proof reading, though any mistakes fall solely on me.

About the Author

While experiencing the typical adventures of growing up, Carrie Dalby called several places in California home, but she's lived on the Alabama Gulf Coast since 1996. Serving two terms as president of Mobile Writers' Guild, five years as the Mobile area Local Liaison for the Society of Children's Book Writers and Illustrators, and helping coordinate the Mobile Literary Festival are some of the writing-related volunteer positions she's held. When Carrie isn't reading, writing, browsing bookstores/libraries, or homeschooling her children, she can often be found knitting or attending concerts.

Carrie writes for both teens and adults. *Fortitude* is listed as a Best Historical Book for Kids by Grateful American Foundation. The Possession Chronicles and The Malevolent Trilogy are her Southern Gothic family saga series for adults. She has also published several short stories that can be found in different anthologies.

For more information, social media links, and news, visit Carrie Dalby's website:

carriedalby.com

9 781957 892245